"What are you doing?"

Canton asked. He noticed the computer and printer for the first time. His eyes narrowed.

"I'm writing a bestselling novel," Janine answered honestly. "It's going to be great," she continued. "It's all about—"

He held up a big hand. "Spare me," he said. "I don't really want to hear the sordid details. No doubt you can draw plenty of material from your years in the commune."

"Why, yes, I can," she agreed with a vacant smile. "But I was going to say that this book is about a pompous businessman with delusions of grandeur."

His eyebrows rose. "How interesting." He stuck his hands into his pockets and she fought a growing attraction to him.

"Don't you have a business empire to save, or something?" she asked irritably.

His eyes slid up and down her slender body. He didn't answer her question. Instead he had one of his own. "How old are you?"

"Twenty-four," she said in a strangled voice.

"And you've told me that you've had more than a handful of lovers, and that boy is your son."

She wasn't listening. Her eyes were on his mouth.

"If you're the mother of a twelve-year-old," he whispered deeply, "I'm a cactus plant!"

Dear Reader,

In 1993 beloved, bestselling author Diana Palmer launched the FABULOUS FATHERS series with *Emmett* (SR#910), which was her 50th Silhouette book. Readers fell in love with that Long, Tall Texan who discovered the meaning of love and fatherhood, and ever since, the FABULOUS FATHERS series has been a favorite. And now, to celebrate the publication of the *50th* FABULOUS FATHERS book, Silhouette Romance is very proud to present a brand-new novel by Diana Palmer, *Mystery Man,* and Fabulous Father Canton Rourke.

Silhouette Romance is just chock-full of special books this month! We've got *Miss Maxwell Becomes a Mom,* book one of Donna Clayton's new miniseries, THE SINGLE DADDY CLUB. And Alice Sharpe's *Missing: One Bride* is book one of our SURPRISE BRIDES trio, three irresistible books by three wonderful authors about very unusual wedding situations.

Rounding out the month is Jodi O'Donnell's newest title, *Real Marriage Material,* in which a sexy man of the land gets tamed. Robin Wells's *Husband and Wife...Again* tells the tale of a divorced couple reuniting in a delightful way. And finally, in *Daddy for Hire* by Joey Light, a hunk of a man becomes the most muscular nanny there ever was, all for love of his little girl.

Enjoy Diana Palmer's *Mystery Man* and all of our wonderful books this month. There's just no better way to start off springtime than with six books bursting with love!

Regards,

Melissa Senate
Senior Editor
Silhouette Books

Please address questions and book requests to:
Silhouette Reader Service
U.S.: 3010 Walden Ave., P.O. Box 1325, Buffalo, NY 14269
Canadian: P.O. Box 609, Fort Erie, Ont. L2A 5X3

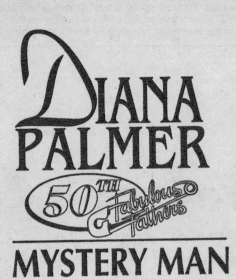

DIANA PALMER

50TH Fabulous Fathers

MYSTERY MAN

Silhouette
ROMANCE™
Published by Silhouette Books
America's Publisher of Contemporary Romance

For M.A.

SILHOUETTE BOOKS

ISBN 0-373-19210-X

MYSTERY MAN

Copyright © 1997 by Diana Palmer

Dear Reader,

I didn't realize this until my editor, Tara Gavin,
pointed it out, but my 50th book was the very first
FABULOUS FATHER, and here I am doing the 50th
FABULOUS FATHER. Talk about nice coincidences!
I love this series, and it's a pleasure to have been included
in it once more!

This book has been hilarious to write, particularly because
the part about an author having a crush on the sexy villain
in a really neat science fiction series happens to be true. I
am happily married with a teenaged son, I hasten to add,
and I do have a life. But we all get caught up in fantasy
from time to time.

I had a ball doing this book, and I hope you enjoy the
result. Now you'll have to excuse me, because they're
rerunning an episode of that neat science fiction show, and
it just happens to feature that very masculine villain....

Love,
Diana Palmer

Chapter One

"It was a dark and stormy night..."

A pair of green eyes glared at the twelve-year-old boy by the window who intoned the trite words in a ghostly voice.

He shrugged. "Well, everybody starts a murder mystery that way, Janie," Kurt Curtis told his older sister with a grin.

Janine ran restless fingers through her short black hair, muttering at the few words on her computer screen. "I don't," she murmured absently. "That's why I sell so many of them."

"Diane Woody," he intoned, "bestselling authoress of the famous Diane Woody Mystery series." He scowled. "Why do you use your pen name for your main character's name? Isn't that redundant?"

"It was the publisher's idea. Could you ask questions later?" she mumbled. "I'm stuck for a line."

"I just gave you one," he reminded her, grinning wider. He was redheaded and blue-eyed, so different from her in coloring that most people thought he was someone else's brother. He was, however, the image of their maternal grandfather. Recessive genes will out, their archaeologist parents were fond of saying.

Their parents were on a new dig, which was why Janine was in Cancún working, with Kurt driving her nuts. Dan and Joan Curtis, both professors at Indiana University, were in the Yucatán on a dig. There had been several other archaeologists on the team, most of whom had to return to take classes. Since this was a newly discovered, and apparently untouched, Mayan site, the Curtises had taken a temporary leave of absence from their teaching positions to pursue it. It wasn't feasible to take Kurt, who was just getting over a bad case of tonsillitis, into the júngles. Neither could they leave him in the exclusive boarding school he attended.

So they'd taken him out of his boarding school for two months—with the proviso that Janine tutor him at home. They'd rented this nice beach house for Janine, where she could meet her publisher's deadline and take care of her little brother. He was well now, but she had him for the duration, which could easily mean another month, and she had to juggle his homebound school assignments with her obligations. The dig was going extremely well, Professor Curtis had said in his last E-mail message through the computer satellite hookup at their camp, and promised to be a site of international importance.

Janine supposed it would be. The benefit of it all was that they had this gorgeous little villa in Cancún overlooking the beach. Janine could write and hear the roar of the ocean outside. It gave her inspiration, usually. When Kurt wasn't trying to "help" her, that was.

She was just slightly nervous, though, because it was September and the tail end of hurricane season, and this had been a year for hurricanes. One prognosticator called it the year of the killer winds. Poetic. And frightening. So far there hadn't been too much to worry them here. She prayed there wouldn't be any more hurricanes. After all, it was almost October.

"Did you notice the new people next door?" Kurt asked. "There's a tall, sour-looking man and a girl about my age. He's never home and she sits on their deck just staring at the ocean."

"You know I don't have time for neighbors," she murmured as she stared at the screen.

"Don't you ever stop and smell the flowers?" he asked with disgust. "You'll be an old maid if you keep this up."

"I'll be a *rich* old maid," she replied absently as she scrolled the pages up the screen. "Besides, there's Quentin."

"Quentin Hobard," he muttered, throwing up his hands. "Good Lord, Janie, he teaches ancient history!"

She glared at him. "He teaches *medieval* history, primarily the Renaissance period. If you'd listen to him once in a while, you might discover that he knows a lot about it."

"Like I can't wait to revisit the Spanish Inquisition," he scoffed.

"It wasn't as horrible as those old movies suggest," she said, sitting up to give him her undivided attention.

"I was thinking more along the lines of 'Monty Python,'" he drawled, naming his favorite classic television show. He got up and struck a pose. "Nobody escapes the Spanish Inquisition!"

She threw up her hands. "You can't learn history from a British comedy show!"

"Sure you can." He leaned forward, grinning. "Want to know the *real* story of the knights? They used coconut shells for horses—"

"I don't want to hear it," she said, and covered her ears. "Let me work or we're both going to starve."

"Not hardly," he said with confidence. "There's always royalties."

"Twelve, and you're an investment counselor."

"I learned all I know from you. I'm precocious on account of the fact that I'm the youngest child of scientists."

"You'd be precocious if you were the youngest child of Neanderthals."

"Did you know that the *h* in Neanderthals is silent and unpronounced? It was written wrong. It's a German word," he continued.

She held up a hand and her glare grew. "I don't need lessons in pronunciation. *I need peace and quiet!*"

"Okay, I get the message! I'll go out and fish for sea serpents."

She didn't even glance his way. "Great. If you catch one, yell. I'll take photos."

"It would serve you right if I did."

"Yes. With your luck, if you caught one, it would eat you, and I'd spend the rest of my life on this beach with a lantern like Heathcliff roaming the moors."

"Wrong storyline. I'm your brother, not your girlfriend."

"Picky, picky."

He made a face and opened the sliding glass door.

"Close it!" she yelled. "You're letting the cold air out!"

"God forbid!" he gasped. He turned back toward her with bright eyes. "Hey, I just had an idea. Want to know how we could start global cooling? We could have everybody turn on their air conditioners and open all their doors and windows..."

She threw a legal pad in his general direction. Not being slow on the uptake, he quickly closed the sliding door and walked down the steps of the deck onto the sugar-white sand on the beach.

He stuck his hands into his pockets and walked toward the house next door, where a skinny young girl sat on the deck, wearing cutoffs with a tank top and an Atlanta Braves hat turned backward. Her bare feet were propped on the rail and she looked out of sorts.

"Hey!" he called.

She glared at him.

"Want to go fishing for sea serpents?" he asked.

Her eyebrows lifted. She smiled, and her whole face changed. She jumped up and bounced down the steps toward him. She was blond and blue-eyed with a fair complexion.

"You're kidding, right?" she asked.

He shrugged. "Ever seen anyone catch a sea serpent around here?"

"Not since we got off the plane," she said.

"Great!" He grinned at her, making his freckles stand out.

"Great?"

"If nobody's caught it, it's still out there!" he whispered, gesturing toward the ocean. "Just think of the residuals from it. We could sell it to one of the grocery store tabloids and clean up!"

Her eyes brightened. "What a neat idea."

"Sure it is." He sighed. "If only I knew how to make one."

"A mop," she ventured. "A dead fish. Parts of some organ meat. A few feathers. A garden hose, some shears and some gray paint."

A kindred soul. He was in heaven. "You're a genius!"

She grinned back. "My dad really is a genius. He taught me everything I know." She sighed. "But if we create a hoax, I'll be grounded for the rest of my life. So I guess I'll pass, but..."

He made a face. "I know what you mean. I'd never live it down. My parents would send me to military school."

"Would they, really?"

"They threaten me with it every time I get into trouble. I don't mind boarding school, but I hate uniforms!"

"Me, too, unless they're baseball uniforms. This year is it, this is the third time, this is the charm. This time," she assured him, "the Braves are going to go all the way!"

He gave her a long, thoughtful look. "Well, we'll see."

"You a Braves fan?" she asked.

He hadn't ever cared much for baseball, but it seemed important to her. "Sure," he said.

She chuckled. "My name is Karie."

"I'm Kurt."

"Nice to meet you."

"Same here."

They walked along the beach for a minute or two. He stopped and looked back up the deserted stretch of land. "Know where to find a mop?" he asked after a minute.

Blissfully unaware that her young brother had just doubled his potential for disaster, Janine filled her computer screen with what she hoped was going to be the bare bones of a new mystery. Some books almost wrote themselves. Others were on a par with pulling teeth. This looked like one of those. Her mind was tired. It wanted to shape clouds into white horses and ocean waves into pirate ships.

"What I need," she said with a sigh, "is a good dose of fantasy."

Sadly there wasn't anything on television that she wanted to watch. Most of it, she couldn't understand, because it was in Spanish.

She turned the set off. The one misery of this trip was missing her favorite weekly science fiction series. Not that she didn't like all the characters on it; she did. But her favorite was an arrogant, sometimes very devious alien commander. The bad guy. She seemed to be spending all her productive time lately sighing over him instead of doing the work that she got paid to do. That was one reason she'd agreed to come to Cancún with her parents and Kurt, to get away from the make-believe man who was ruining her writing career.

"Enough of this!" she muttered to herself. "Good heavens, you'd think I was back in grammar school, idolizing teachers!"

She got up and paced the room. She ate some cookies. She typed a little into the computer. Eventually the sun started going down and she noticed that she was short one twelve-year-old boy.

She looked at her watch. Surely he hadn't gotten the time confused? It was earlier here than in Bloomington, Indiana, where Kurt lived with their parents. Had he mistaken the time, perhaps forgotten to reset his watch? Janine frowned, hoping that she hadn't forgotten to set her own. It would be an hour behind Kurt's, because her apartment in Chicago was in a different time zone from Kurt and her parents' in Indiana.

He was in a foreign country and he didn't speak any more Spanish than she did. Their parents' facility for languages had escaped them, for the most part. Janine spoke German with some fluency, but not much Spanish. And while English was widely spoken here in the hotels and tourist spots, on the street it was a different story. Many of the local people in Cancún still spoke Mayan and considered Spanish, not English, a second language.

She turned off her computer—it was useless trying to work when she was worried, anyway—and went out to the beach. She found the distinctive tread of Kurt's sneakers and followed them in the damp sand where the tide hadn't yet reached. The sun was low on the horizon and the wind was up. There were dark clouds all around. She never forgot the danger of hurricanes here, and even if it was late September, that didn't mean a hurricane was no longer a possibility.

She shaded her eyes against the glare of the sun, because she was walking west across the beach, stopping when Kurt's sneakers were joined by another, smaller pair, with no discernible tread. She knelt down, scowling as she studied the track. She'd worked as a private eye for a couple of years, but any novice would figure out that these were the footprints of a girl, she thought. The girl Kurt had mentioned, perhaps, the one who lived next door. In fact, she was almost in front of that beach house now.

The roar of the waves had muffled the sound of approaching footsteps. One minute, she was staring down at the tracks. The next, she was looking at a large and highly polished pair of black dress shoes. Tapered neatly around them were the hem of expensive slacks. The legs seemed to go up forever. Far above them, glaring down at her, were pale blue eyes under a jutting brow in a long, lean face. The lips were thin. The top one was long and narrow, the lower one had only a hint of fullness. The cheekbones were high and the nose was long and straight. The hairline was just slightly receding around straight brown hair.

Two enormous lean hands were balled into fists, resting on the hips of the newcomer.

"May I ask what you're doing on my beach?" he asked in a voice like raspy velvet.

She stood up, a little clumsy. How odd, that a total stranger should make her knees weak.

"I'm tracking my..." she began.

"Tracking?" he scoffed, as if he thought she were lying. His blue eyes narrowed. He looked oddly dangerous, as if he never smiled, as if he could move like lightning and would at the least provocation.

Her heart was racing. "His name is Kurt and he's only twelve," she said. "He's redheaded and so high." She made a mark in the air with her flat hand.

"That one," he murmured coolly. "Yes, I've seen him prowling around. Where's my daughter?"

Her eyebrows rose. "You have a daughter? Imagine that! Is she carved out of stone, too?"

His firm, square chin lifted and he looked even more

threatening. "She's missing. I told her not to leave the house."

"If she's with Kurt, she's perfectly safe," she began, about to mention that he'd been stranded once in the middle of Paris by their forgetful parents, and had found his way home to their hotel on the west bank. Not only had he maneuvered around a foreign city, but he'd also sold some of the science fiction cards he always carried with him to earn cab fare, and he'd arrived with twenty dollars in his pocket. Kurt was resourceful.

But long before she could manage any of that, the man moved a step closer and cocked his head. "Do you know where they are?"

"No, but I'm sure..."

"You may let your son run loose like a delinquent, but my daughter knows better," he said contemptuously. His eyes ran over her working attire with something less than admiration. She had on torn, raveled cutoffs that came almost to her knee. With them she was wearing old, worn-out sandals and a torn shirt that didn't even hint at the lovely curves beneath it. Her short hair was windblown. She wasn't even wearing makeup. She could imagine how she looked. What had he said—her *son?*

"Now, just wait a minute here," she began.

"Where's your husband?" he demanded.

Her eyes blazed. "I'm not married!"

Those eyebrows were really expressive now.

She flushed. "My private life is none of your business," she said haughtily. His assumptions, added to his obvious contempt, made her furious. An idea flashed into her mind and, inwardly, she chuckled. She struck a pose, prepared to live right down to his image of her. "But just for the record," she added in purring tones, "my *son* was born in a commune. I'm not really sure who his father is, of course…"

The expression on his face was unforgettable. She wished with all her heart for a camera, so that she could relive the moment again and again.

"A commune? Is that where you learned to track?" he asked pointedly.

"Oh, no." She searched for other outlandish things to tell him. He was obviously anxious to learn any dreadful aspect of her past. "I learned that from a Frenchman that I lived with up in the northern stretches of Canada. He taught me how to track and make coats from the fur of animals." She smiled helpfully. "I can shoot, too."

"Wonderful news for the ammunition industry, no doubt," he said with a mocking smile.

She put her own hands on her hips and glared back. It was a long way up, although she was medium height. "It's getting dark."

"Better track fast, hadn't you?" he added. He lifted a hand and motioned to a man coming down toward the beach. "*¿Sabe donde están?*" he shot at the man in fluent Spanish.

"*No, lo siento, señor. ¡Nadie los han visto!*" the smaller man called back.

"*Llame a la policía.*"

"*Sí, señor!*"

Police sounded the same in any language and her pulse jumped. "You said *police.* You're going to call the police?" she groaned. That was all she needed, to have to explain to a police officer that she'd forgotten the time and let her little brother get lost.

"You speak Spanish?" he asked with some disbelief.

"No, but police sounds the same in most languages, I guess."

"Have you got a better idea?"

She sighed. "No, I guess not. It's just that..."

"Dad!"

They both whirled as Karie and Kurt came running along the beach with an armload of souvenirs between them, wearing sombreros.

"Gosh, Dad, I'm sorry, we forgot the time!" Karie warbled to her father. "We went to the *mercado* in town and bought all this neat stuff. Look at my hat! It's called a sombrero, and I got it for a dollar!"

"Yeah, and look what I got, S—*mmmmffg.*" Kurt's "Sis" was cut off in midstream by Janine's hand across his mouth.

She grinned at him. "That's fine, *son,*" she emphasized, her eyes daring him to contradict her. "You know, you shouldn't really scare your poor old *mother* this way," she added, in case he hadn't gotten the point.

Kurt was intrigued. Obviously his big sister wanted this rather formidable-looking man to think he was her son. Okay. He could go along with a gag. Just in case, he stared at Karie until she got the idea, too, and nodded to let him know that she understood.

"I'm sorry...*Mom,*" Kurt added with an apologetic smile. "But Karie and I were having so much fun, we just forgot the time. And then when we tried to get back, neither of us knew any Spanish, so we couldn't call a cab. We had to find someone who spoke English to get us a cab."

"All the cabdrivers speak enough English to get by," Karie's father said coldly.

"We didn't know that, Dad," Karie defended. "This is my friend Kurt. He lives next door."

Karie's dad didn't seem very impressed with Kurt, either. He stared at his daughter. "I have to stop José before he gets the police out here on a wild-goose chase. And then we have to leave," he told her. "We're having dinner with the Elligers and their daughter."

"Oh, gosh, not them again," she groaned. "Missy wants to marry you."

"Karie," he said warningly.

She sighed. "Oh, all right. Kurt, I guess I'll see you tomorrow."

"Sure thing, Karie."

"Maybe we can find that garden hose," she added in a conspiratorial tone.

He brightened. "Great idea!"

"What the hell do you want with a hose?" Karie's father asked as they walked back up the beach, totally ignoring the two people he'd just left.

"Whew!" Kurt huffed. "Gosh, he's scary!"

"No, he isn't," Janine said irritably. "He's just pompous and irritating! And he thinks he's an emperor or something. I told him we lived in a commune and you're my son and I don't know who your father is. Don't you tell him any differently," she added when he tried to speak. "I want to live down to his image of me!"

He chuckled. "Boy, are you mad," he said. "You don't have fights with anybody."

"Wait," she promised, glaring after the man.

"He reminds me of somebody," he said.

"Probably the devil," she muttered. "I hear he's got blue eyes. Somebody wrote a song about it a few years ago."

"No," he mumbled, still thinking. "Didn't he seem familiar to you?"

"Yes, he did," she admitted. "I don't know why. I've never seen him before."

"Are you kidding? You don't know who he is? Haven't you recognized him? He's famous enough as he is. But just think, Janie, think if he had gray makeup on."

"He could pass for a sand crab," she muttered absently.

"That's not what I meant," he muttered. "Listen, they call this guy Mr. Software. Good grief, don't you ever read the newspapers or watch the news?"

"No. It depresses me," she said, glowering.

He sighed. "Mr. Software just lost everything. For the past year, he's been involved in a lawsuit to prevent a merger that would have saved his empire. He just lost the suit, and a fortune with it. Now he can't merge his software company with a major computer chain. He's down here avoiding the media so he can get himself back together before he starts over again. He's already promised his stockholders that he'll recoup every penny he lost. I bet he will, too. He's a tiger."

She scowled. "He, who?"

"Him. Canton Rourke," he emphasized. "Third generation American, grandson of Irish immigrants. His mother was Spanish, can't you tell it in his bearing? He made billions designing and selling computer programs, and now he's moving into computer production. The company he was trying to acquire made the computer you use. And the software word processing program you use was one he designed himself."

"That's Canton Rourke?" she asked, turning to stare at the already dim figure in the distance. "I thought he was much older than that."

"He's old enough, I guess. He's divorced. Karie said her mother ran for the hills when it looked like he was going to risk everything in that merger attempt. She likes jewelry and real estate and high living. She found herself another rich man and remarried within a month of the divorce becoming final. She moved to Greece. Just as well, probably. Her parents were never together, anyway. He was always working on a program and her mother was at some party, living it up. What a mismatch!"

"I guess so." She shook her head. "He didn't look like a billionaire."

"He isn't, now. All he has is his savings, from what they say on TV, and that's not a whole lot."

"That sort of man will make it all back," she said thoughtfully. "Workaholics make money because they love to work. Most of them don't care much about the money, though. That's just how they keep score."

His eyes narrowed. "You still haven't guessed why he looks familiar."

She turned and scowled at him. "You said something about gray makeup?"

"Sure. Think," he added impatiently. "Those eyes. That deep, smooth voice. Where do you hear them every fourth or fifth week?"

"On the news?"

He chuckled. "Only if they had aliens doing it."

His rambling was beginning to make sense. Every

fourth or fifth week, there was a guest star on her favorite science fiction show. Her heartbeat increased alarmingly. Her breath caught in her throat. She put a hand there, to make sure she was still breathing.

"Oh, no." She shook her head. She smiled nervously. "No, he doesn't look like *him!*"

"He most certainly does," Kurt said confidently. "Same height, build, eyes, bone structure, even the same deep sort of voice." He nodded contemplatively. "What a coincidence, huh? We came here to Mexico to get you away from the television so you could write without being distracted by your favorite villain. And his doppelgänger turns up here on the beach!"

Chapter Two

"I don't like having you around that boy," Canton told his daughter when they were back in their beach house. "His mother is a flake."

Karie had to bite her tongue to keep from blurting out the truth. Obviously the Curtis duo didn't want it known that they were little brother and big sister, not son and mother. Karie would keep her new friend's secret, but it wasn't going to be easy.

Her eyes went to the new hardcover murder mystery on the coffee table. There was a neat brown leather bookmark holding Canton's place in it. On the cover in huge red block letters were the title, "CATA-COMB," and the author's name—Diane Woody.

There was a photo in the back of the book, on the slick jacket, but it was of a woman with long hair and dark glasses wearing a hat with a big brim. It didn't even look like their neighbor. But it was. Karie knew because Kurt had told her, with some pride, who his sister was. She was thrilled to know, even secondhand, a big-time mystery writer like Diane Woody. Her father was one of the biggest fans of the bestselling mystery author, but he wouldn't recognize her from that book jacket. Maybe it was a good thing. Apparently she didn't want to be recognized.

"Kurt's nice," she told her father. "He's twelve. He likes people. He's honest and kind. And Janine's nice, too."

His eyebrows lifted as he glanced at her over his shoulder. "Janine?" he murmured, involuntarily liking the sound of the name on his lips.

"His...mother."

"You learned all that about him in one day?"

She shrugged. "Actions speak louder than words, isn't that what you always say?"

His face softened, just a little. He loved his daughter. "Just don't go wandering off with him again, okay?"

"Okay."

"And don't go to his home," he added through his teeth. "Because even if he can't help what he's got for a mother, I don't want you associating with her. Is that clear?"

"Oh, yes, sir!"

"Good. Get dressed. We don't have much time."

In the days that followed, Kurt and Karie were inseparable. Karie, as usual, agreed with whatever her father told her to do and then did what she pleased. He was so busy trying to regroup that he usually forgot his orders five minutes after he gave them, anyway.

So Karie and Kurt concocted their "sea serpent," piece by painstaking piece, concealing it under the Rourke beach house for safety. Meanwhile, they watched World War III develop between their respective relatives.

The first salvo came suddenly and without warning. Kurt had gone out to play baseball with Karie. This was something new for him. His parents were studious and bookwormish, not athletic. And even though Janine was more than willing to share the occasional game of ball toss, she wasn't a baseball fanatic. Kurt had grown to his present age without much tutoring in sports, except what he played at the private school where his parents sent him. And that was precious little, because the owners were too wary of lawsuits to let the children do much rough-and-tumble stuff.

Karie had no hang-ups at all about playing tackle football on the beach or smacking a hardball with her regulation bat. She gave the bat to Kurt and told him to do his best. Unfortunately, he did, on the very first try.

Canton Rourke came storming up onto the porch of the beach house and right onto the open patio without a knock. Janine, lost in the fifth chapter of her new book, was so foggy that she saw him without really seeing him. She was in the middle of a chase scene, locked into character and time and place, totally mindless and floating in the computer screen. She stared at him blankly.

He looked furious. The blue eyes under that jutting brow were blazing from his lean face. He had a hardball in one hand. He stuck it under her nose.

"It's a baseball," she said helpfully.

"I know what the damned thing is," he said in a tone that would have affected her if she hadn't been deep in concentration. "I just picked it up off my living-room floor. It went through the bay window."

"You shouldn't let the kids play baseball in the house," she instructed.

"They weren't playing in the damned house! Your son slammed it through the window!"

Her eyebrows rose. Things were beginning to focus in the real world. Her mind lost the last thread of connection with her plot. Before she lost her bearings too far, she saved the file before she swung her chair back to face her angry neighbor.

"Nonsense," she said. "Kurt doesn't have a baseball. Come to think of it, I don't think he knows how to use a bat, either."

He threw the ball up and caught it, deliberately.

"All right, what do you want me to do about it?" she asked wearily.

"I want you to teach him not to hit balls through people's windows," he said shortly. "It's a damned nuisance trying to find a glass company down here, especially one that can get a repair done quickly."

"Put some plastic over the hole with tape," she suggested.

"Your son did the damage," he continued with a mocking smile. "The repair is going to be up to you, not me."

"*Me?*"

"You." He put the ball down firmly on her desk, noticing the computer and printer for the first time. His eyes narrowed. "What are you doing?"

"I'm writing a bestselling novel," she said honestly.

He laughed without humor. "Sure."

"It's going to be great," she continued with building anger. "It's all about a—"

He held up a big, lean hand. "Spare me," he said. "I don't really want to hear the sordid details. No doubt you can draw plenty of material from your years in the commune."

"Why, yes, I can," she agreed with a vacant smile. "But I was going to say that this book is about a pompous businessman with delusions of grandeur."

His eyebrows lifted. "How interesting." He stuck his hands into his pockets and she fought a growing attraction to him. He really did have an extraordinary build for a man his age, which looked to be late thirties. He was lean and muscular and sensuous. He didn't have a male-model sort of look, but there was something in the very set of his head, in the way he looked at her, that made her knees go weak.

His eye had been caught by an autographed photo peering out from under her mousepad. She'd hidden it there so that Kurt wouldn't see it and tease her about her infatuation with her television hero. Sadly when she'd moved the mouse to save her file, she'd shifted the pad and revealed the photo.

His lean hand reached out and tugged at the corner. He didn't wear jewelry of any kind, she noticed, and his fingernails were neatly trimmed and immaculate. He had beautiful hands, lightly tanned and strong.

"I like to watch the television series he's in," she said defensively, because he was staring intently at the photo.

His gaze lifted and he laughed softly. "Do you?" He handed it back and in the process, leaned close to her. "It's one of my favorite shows, too," he said, his voice dropping an octave, soft and deep and sensuous. "But this is the villain, you know, not the hero."

She cleared her throat. He was close enough to make her uncomfortable. "So what?"

"He looks familiar, doesn't he?" he murmured dryly.

She glared up at him. He really was far too close. Her heart skipped. "Does he?" she asked. Her voice sounded absolutely squeaky.

He stood up again, his hands back in his pockets, his smile so damned arrogant and knowing that she could have kicked him.

"Don't you have a business empire to save or something?" she asked irritably.

"I suppose so. You can't get that show down here, at least not in English," he added.

"Yes. I know. That was the whole purpose of coming here," she murmured absently.

"Ah, I see. Drying out, are we?"

She stood up. "You listen here…!"

He chuckled. "I have things to do. You'll see to the window, of course."

She took a steadying breath. "Of course."

His eyes slid up and down her slender body with more than a little interest. "Odd."

"What?"

"Do you mind if I test a theory?"

Her eyes were wary. "What sort of theory?"

He took his hands out of his pockets and moved close, very deliberately, his eyes staring straight into hers the whole while. When he was right up against her, almost touching her, he stopped. His hands remained at his side. He never touched her. But his eyes, his beautiful blue eyes, stared right down into hers and suddenly slipped to her mouth, tracing it with such sensuality that her lips parted on a shaky breath.

He moved again. His chest was touching her breasts now. She could smell the clean, sexy scent he wore. She could feel his warm, coffee-scented breath on her mouth as he breathed.

"How old are you?" he asked in a deep, sultry tone.

"Twenty-four," she said in a strangled voice.

"Twenty-four." He bent his head, so that his mouth was poised just above hers, tantalizing but not invasive, not aggressive at all. His breath made little patterns on her parted lips. "And you've had more than a handful of lovers?"

She wasn't listening. Her eyes were on his mouth. It looked firm and hard and very capable. She wondered how it tasted. She wondered. She wished. She...wanted!

"Janine."

The sound of her voice on his lips brought her wide, curious eyes up to meet his. They looked stunned, mesmerized.

His own eyes crinkled, as if he were smiling. All she saw was the warmth in them.

"If you're the mother of a twelve-year-old," he whispered deeply, "I'm a cactus plant."

He lifted his head, gave her an amused, indulgent smile, turned and walked away without a single word or a backward glance, leaving her holding the ball. In more ways than one.

She got the glass fixed. It wasn't easy, but she managed. However, she did dare Kurt to pick up a bat again.

"You don't like him, do you?" he queried the day

after the glass was repaired. "Why not? He seems to be good to Karie, and he isn't exactly Mr. Nasty to me, either."

She moved restlessly. "I'm trying to work," she said evasively. She didn't like to remember her last encounter with their neighbor. Weakness was dangerous around that tiger.

"He's gone to California," Kurt added.

Her fingers jumped on the keyboard, scattering letters across the screen. "Oh. Has he?"

"He's going to talk to some people in Silicon Valley. I'll bet he'll make it right back to where he was before he's through. His wife is going to be real sorry that she ran out on him when he lost it all."

"No foresight," she agreed. She saved the file. There was no sense working while Kurt was chattering away. She got up and stretched, moving to the patio window. She paused there, staring curiously. Karie was sitting on the beach on a towel. Nearby, a man stood watching her; a very dark man with sunglasses on and a suspicious look about him.

"Who's that? Have you seen him before?" she asked Kurt.

He glanced out. "Yes. He was out there yesterday."

"Who's watching Karie while her father's gone?"

"I think there's a housekeeper who cooks for them," he said. "He's only away for the day, though."

"That's long enough for a kidnapper," she said quietly. "He was very wealthy. Maybe someone wouldn't know that, would make a try for Karie."

"You mystery writers," Kurt scoffed, "always looking on the dark side."

"Dark side or not, he isn't hurting Karie while I'm

around!'' She went right out the patio door and down the steps.

She walked toward the man. He saw her coming, and stepped back, looking as if he wasn't sure what to do.

She went right up to him, aware that her two years of martial arts training might not be enough if he turned nasty. Well, she could always scream, and the beach was fairly crowded today.

''You're on my property. What do you want?'' she asked the man, who was tall and well-built and foreign looking.

His eyebrows rose above his sunglasses. ''*No hablo inglés,*'' he said, and grinned broadly.

She knew very little Spanish, but that phrase was one she'd had to learn. ''And I don't speak Spanish,'' she returned with a sigh. ''Well, you have to go. Go away. Away! Away!'' She made a flapping gesture with her hand.

''Ah. *¡Vaya!*'' he said obligingly.

''That's right. *Vaya.* Right now.''

He nodded, grinned again and went back down the beach in the opposite direction.

Janine watched him walk away. She had a nagging suspicion that he wasn't hanging around here for his health.

She went down the beach to where Karie was sitting, spellbound at the scene she'd just witnessed. ''Karie, I want you to come and stay with Kurt and me today while your dad's gone,'' she said. ''I don't like the way that man was watching you.''

''Neither do I,'' Karie had to admit. She smiled ruefully. ''Dad had a bodyguard back in Chicago. I never really got used to him. Down here it's been quieter.''

"You do have a bodyguard. Me."

Karie chuckled as she got up and shook out her towel. "I noticed. You weren't scared of him at all, were you?"

"Kurt and I studied martial arts for two years. I'm pretty good at it." She'd didn't add that she'd also worked as a private investigator.

"Would you teach me?"

"That might not be a bad idea," she considered. "Tell you what, Kurt and I will give you lessons on the sly. You may not want to share that with your dad right now. He's mad enough about the window at the moment."

"Dad isn't mean," Karie replied. "He's pretty cool, most of the time. He has a terrible temper, of course."

"I noticed."

Karie smiled. "You have one, too. That man started backing up the minute you went toward him. You scared him."

"Why, so I did," Janine mused. She grinned with pride. "How about that?"

"I'm starved," Karie said. "Maria went to the grocery store and she won't be back for hours."

"We'll make sandwiches. I've got cake, too, for dessert. Coconut."

"Wow! Radical!"

Janine smiled. She led the way back to the beach house, where an amused Kurt was waiting.

"Diane Woody to the rescue!" he chuckled.

She made a face at him. "I'm reading too much of my own publicity," she conceded. "But the man left, didn't he?"

"Left a jet trail behind him," her brother agreed.

"What are you working on...oh! It's *him!*" Karie

gasped, picking up the photo of the television star in makeup that Janine had left on the desk. "Isn't he cool? It's my favorite show. I like the captain best, but this guy isn't so bad. He sort of looks like Dad, you know?"

Janine didn't say a word. But inside, she groaned.

She was feeding the kids coconut cake from a local store, and milk when a familiar threatening presence came through the patio doors without knocking. She gave him a glare that he simply ignored.

"Don't you live at home anymore?" he asked his daughter irritably.

"There's no cake at our place," Karie said matter-of-factly.

"Where's the housekeeper? I told her to stay with you."

"She went shopping and never came back," Janine said shortly. "Your daughter was on the beach being watched by a very suspicious-looking man."

"Janine scared him off," Karie offered, with a toothy grin. "She knows karate!"

The arrogant look that Canton Rourke gave her was unsettling. "Karate, hmmm?"

"I know a little," she confessed.

"She went right up to that man and told him to go away," Karie continued, unabashed. "Then she took me home with her." She glowered at him. "I could have been kidnapped!"

He looked strange for a space of seconds, as if he couldn't quite get his bearings.

"You shouldn't have been out there alone," he said finally.

"I was just lying on my beach towel."

"Well, from now on, lie on the deck," he replied curtly. "No more adventures."

"Okay," she said easily, and ate another chunk of cake.

"It's coconut cake," Kurt volunteered. "That little grocery store has them. Janie gets them all the time for us. They're great."

"I'd offer you a slice of cake, Mr. Rourke, but I'm sure you're in a terrible hurry."

"I suppose I must be. Come on, Karie."

His daughter took a big swallow of milk and got up from the table. "Thanks, Janie!"

"You're very welcome." She glanced at Canton. "Housekeepers don't make very good bodyguards."

"I never meant her to be a watchdog, only a cook and housecleaner. Apparently I'd better look elsewhere."

"It might be wise."

His eyes slid down her long legs in worn jeans, down to her bare, pretty feet. He smiled in spite of himself. "Don't like shoes, hmmm?"

"Shoes wear out. Skin doesn't."

He chuckled. "You sound like Einstein. I recall reading that he never wore socks, for the same reason."

Her eyes lifted to his face and slid over it with that same sense of stomach-rapping excitement that she experienced the first time she saw it. He did so closely resemble her favorite series TV character. It was uncanny, really.

"Are you sure you don't act?" she asked without meaning to.

He gave her a wry look. "I'm sure. And I'm not about to start, at my age."

"There go your hopes, dashed for good," Kurt murmured dryly. "He's not an illegal alien trying to fit in with humans, Janie. Tough luck."

She flushed. "Will you shut up!"

"What did you do with that autographed photo?" he asked as he passed the desk.

"Oh, she never has it out when she's working," Kurt volunteered. "If she can see it, she just sits and sighs over it and never gets a word on the screen."

He scowled, interested. "What sort of work do you do?"

"She's a secretary," Kurt said for her, gleefully improvising. "Her boss is a real slave driver, so even on vacation, she has to take the computer with her so that she can use the computer's fax modem to send her work to the office."

He made an irritated sound. "Some boss."

"He pays well," she said, warming to Kurt's improvisation. She sighed. "You know how it is, living in a commune, you get so out of touch with reality." She contrived to look dreamy-eyed. "But eventually, one has to return to the real world and earn a living. It really is so hard to get used to material things again."

His face closed up. He gave her a glare that could have stopped traffic and motioned to Karie to follow him. He stuck his hands into his pockets and walked out the door. He never looked back. It seemed to be a deep-seated characteristic.

Karie grinned and waved, following obediently.

When they were out of sight along the beach, Kurt joined her on the patio deck.

"What if that man wasn't watching Karie at all?" she wondered aloud, having had time to formulate a different theory. "What if he's a lookout for the pot-hunters?"

Kurt scowled. "You mean those people who steal artifacts from archaeological sites and sell them on the black market?"

"The very same." She folded her arms over her T-shirt. "This is a brand-new site, unexplored and uncharted until now. Mom and Dad even noted that it seemed to be totally undisturbed. The Maya did some exquisite work with gold and precious jewels. What if there's a king's ransom located at the dig and someone knows about it?"

Kurt leaned against the railing. "They know it can happen. It did last time they found a site deep in the jungle, over near Chichén Itzá. But they had militia guarding them and the pothunters were caught."

"Yes, but Mexico is hurting for money, and it's hard to keep militia on a site all the time to guard a few archaeologists."

"Dad has a gun."

"And he can shoot it. Sure he can. But they can't stay awake twenty-four hours a day, and even militia can be bribed."

"You're a whale of a comfort," Kurt groaned.

"I'm sorry. I just think we should be on our guard. It could have been someone trying to kidnap Karie, but they've just as much incentive to kidnap us or at least keep a careful eye on us."

"In other words, we'd better watch our backs."

Janine smiled. "Exactly."

"Suits me." He sighed. "What a shame your alien hero can't beam down here and help us out. I'll bet he'd have the bad guys for breakfast."

"Oh, they don't eat humans," she assured him.

"They might make an exception for pothunters."

"You do have a point there. Come on. You can help me do the dishes."

"Tell you what," he said irrepressibly. "You do the dishes, and I'll write your next chapter for you!"

"Be my guest."

He gave her a wary look. "You're kidding, right?"

"Wrong. Go for it."

He was excited, elated. He took her at her word and went straight to the computer. He loaded her word processing program, pulled up the file where she'd left off, scanned the plot.

He sat and he sat and he sat. By the time she finished cleaning up the kitchen, he was still sitting.

"Nothing yet?" she asked.

He gave her a plaintive stare. "How do you *do* this?" he groaned. "I can't even think of a single word to put on paper!"

"Thinking is the one thing I don't do," she told him. "Move."

He got up and she sat down. She stared at the screen for just a minute, checked her place in the plot, put her fingers on the keyboard and just started typing. She was two pages into the new scene when Kurt let out a long sigh and walked away.

"Writers," he said, "are strange."

She chuckled to herself. "You don't know the half of it," she assured him, and kept right on typing.

Chapter Three

Janine was well into the book two days later when Karie came flying up the steps and in through the sliding glass doors.

"We're having a party!" she announced breathlessly. "And you're both invited."

Janine's mind was still in limbo, in the middle of a scene. She gave Karie a vacant stare.

"Oops! Sorry!" Karie said, having already learned in a space of days that writers can't withdraw immediately when they're deep into a scene. She backed out and went to find Kurt.

"What sort of party?" he asked when she joined him at the bottom of the steps at the beach.

"Just for a few of Dad's friends, but I persuaded him to invite you and Janie, too. He feels guilty since he's had to leave me alone so much for the past few years. So he lets me have my way a lot, to try and make it up to me." She grinned at Kurt. "It's sort of like having my own genie."

"You're blackmailing him."

She laughed. "Exactly!"

His thin shoulders rose and fell. "I wouldn't mind coming to the party, if you're having something nice to eat. But Janie won't," he added with certainty. "She hates parties and socializing. And she doesn't like your dad at all, can't you tell?"

"He doesn't like her much, either, but that's no reason why they can't be civil to each other at a party."

"I don't know about that."

"I do. He'll be on his best behavior. Did you know that he reads her books? He doesn't know who she really is, of course, because I haven't told him. But he's got every book she's ever written."

"Good grief, didn't he look at her picture on the book jacket?" Kurt burst out.

"I didn't recognize her from it. Neither will he. It doesn't really look like her, does it?"

He had to admit it didn't. "She doesn't like being recognized," he confided. "It embarrasses her. She likes to write books, but she's not much on publicity."

"Why?"

"She's shy, can you believe it?" he chuckled. "She runs the other way from interviews and conventions and publicity. It drove the publishing house nuts at first, but they finally found a way to capitalize on her eccentricity. They've made her into the original mystery woman. Nobody knows much about her, so she fascinates her reading public."

"I love her books."

"So do I," Kurt said, "but don't ever tell her I said so. We wouldn't want her to get conceited."

She folded her arms on her knees and stared out to sea. "Does she have a, like, boyfriend?"

He groaned. "Yes, if you could call him that. He's a college professor. He teaches ancient history." He made a gagging gesture.

"Is he nice?"

"He's indescribable," he said after thinking about it for a minute.

"Are they going to get married?"

He shrugged. "I hope not. He's really nice, but he thinks Janie should be less flaky. I don't. I like her just the way she is, without any changes. He thinks she's not dignified enough."

"Why?"

"He's very conservative. Nice, but conservative. I don't think he really approves of our parents, either. They're eccentric, too."

She turned to look at him. "What do they do?"

"They're archaeologists," he said. "Both of them teach at Indiana University, where they got their doctorates. We live in Bloomington, Indiana, but Janie lives in Chicago."

"They're both doctors?"

He nodded and made a face. "Yes. Even Janie has a degree, although hers is in history and it's a bachelor of arts. I guess I'll be gang-pressed into going to college. I don't want to."

"What do you want to do?"

He sighed. "I want to fly," he said, looking skyward as a bird, probably a tern, dipped and swept in the wind currents, paying no attention to the odd creatures sitting on the steps below him.

"We could glue some feathers together," she suggested.

"No! I want to fly," he emphasized. "Airplanes, helicopters, anything, with or without wings. It's in my blood. I can't get enough of airplane movies. Even space shows. Now, that's really flying, when you do it in space!''

"So that's why you like that science fiction show Janie's so crazy about."

"Sort of. But I like the action, too."

She smiled. "I like it because the bad guy looks like my dad."

He burst out laughing. "He's not the bad guy. He's the other side."

"Right. The enemy."

"He's not so bad. He saved the hero, once."

"Well, so he did. I guess maybe he isn't all bad."

"He's just misunderstood," he agreed.

She chuckled. They were quiet for a minute or two. "Will you try to get Janie to come to our party?"

He smiled. "I'll give it my best shot. Just don't expect miracles, okay?"

She smiled back. "Okay!"

As it turned out, Janine had to go to the Rourke party, because for once her little brother dug in his heels and insisted on going somewhere. He would, he told her firmly, go alone if she didn't care to go with him.

The thought of her little brother in the sort of company the Rourkes would keep made her very nervous. She didn't socialize enough to know much about people who lived in the fast lane, and she'd never known any millionaires. She was aware that some drank and used drugs. Her sheltered life hadn't prepared her for that kind of company. Now she was going to be thrust into the very thick of it, or so she imagined. Actually she had no idea what Canton's friends were like. Maybe they were down-to-earth and nice.

She hadn't anything appropriate for a cocktail party, but she scrounged up a crinkly black sundress that, when paired with high heels, pearl earrings and a pearl necklace that her parents had given her, didn't look too bad. She brushed her flyaway hair, sprayed it down and went to get her black leather purse.

"I didn't even have enough warning to go and buy a new dress. I hate you," she told Kurt with a sweet smile.

"You'll forgive me. I'll bet when he's dressed up, he's really something to look at," he replied.

"I've seen him dressed up."

"Oh. Well, he's supposed to be the stuff dreams are made of. Karie says half the women in Chicago have thrown themselves at him over the years, especially since his wife remarried."

"They live in Chicago?" She tried to sound disinterested.

"Part of the time," he affirmed. "They have an apartment in New York, too, in downtown Manhattan."

"He may not ever be super rich again," she reminded him.

"That doesn't seem to discourage them," he assured her. "They're all sure that any man who could make it in the first place will be able to get it back."

There was a sort of logic to the assumption, she had to admit. Most men who made that sort of money were workaholics who didn't spare themselves or any of their employees. Given a stake, there was every reason to believe Canton Rourke could rebuild his empire. But she felt sorry for him. He wouldn't ever know who liked him for himself and who liked him for what he had.

"I'm glad I'm not rich," she said aloud.

"What?"

"Oh, I just meant that I know people like me for myself and not for what I've got."

He folded his arms across his neat shirt. "Do go on," he invited. "Tell me about it. What was that invitation you got back home to come to a cocktail party and explain how to get published to the hostess's guest of honor, who just happened to have written a book…?"

She sighed.

"Or the rich lady with the stretch limo who wanted you to get her best friend's book published. Or the mystery writer wannabe who asked for the name of your agent and a recommendation?"

"I quit," she said. "You're right. Everybody has problems."

"So does Mr. Rourke. If you get to know him, you might like him. And there's a fringe benefit."

"There is?"

"Sure. If you nab him, you can buy him a plastic appliance like the one your favorite alien wears and make him over to suit you!"

The thought of Canton Rourke sitting still for that doubled her over with laughter. He'd more than likely give her the appliance face first and tell her where she could go with it.

"I don't really think that would be a good idea," she replied. "Think how his board of directors might react!"

"I suppose so. We should go," he prompted, nodding toward the clock on the side table.

She grimaced. "All right. But I don't want to," she said firmly.

"You'll enjoy yourself," he promised her. "Nobody knows who you are."

She brightened. "I didn't think of that."

"Now you can."

He opened the door for her with a flourish and they walked down the beach through the sand to the Rourke's house. It was ablaze with light and soft music came wafting out the open door of the patio. Several people holding glasses were talking. They all looked exquisitely dressed and Janine already felt self-conscious about her own appearance.

Kurt, oblivious, darted up the steps to his friend Karie, wearing a cute little dress with a dropped waistline and a short skirt that probably had cost more than Janine's summer wardrobe put together. As she went up the steps, she paused to shake the sand out of her high heels, holding onto the bannister for support.

"Need a hand?" a familiar velvety voice asked. A long, lean arm went around her and supported her while she fumbled nervously with her shoe, almost dropping it in the process.

"Here." He knelt and emptied the sand out of the shoe before he eased it back onto her small foot with a sensuality that made her heart race.

He stood up slowly, his eyes meeting hers when they were on the same level, and holding as he rose to his towering height. He didn't smile. For endless seconds, they simply looked at each other.

"This was Kurt's idea," she blurted breathlessly. "I didn't even have time to buy a new dress..."

"What's wrong with this one?" he asked. His lean

hand traced the rounded neckline, barely touching her skin, but she shivered at the contact.

"You, uh, seem to have quite a crowd," she faltered, moving a breath away from him.

"Right now, I wish they were all five hundred miles away," he said deeply, and with an inflection that made her tingle.

She laughed nervously. "Is that a line? If it is, it's probably very effective, but I'm immune. I've got a son and I've lived in a com..."

He held up a hand and chuckled. "Give it up," he advised. "Kurt is twelve and you're twenty-four. I really doubt that you conceived at the age of eleven. As for the commune bit," he added, moving close enough to threaten, "not in your wildest dreams, honey."

Honey. She recalled dumping a glass of milk on a pushy acquaintance who'd used that term in a demeaning way to her. This man made it sound like a verbal caress. Her toes curled.

"Please." Was that her voice, that thin tremulous tone?

His fingers touched her cheek gently. "I'm a new experience, is that it?"

She shivered. "You're a multimillionaire. I'm working for wages." Not quite the truth, but a good enough comparison, she thought frantically.

He leaned closer with a smile that was fascinating. "I gave up seducing girls years ago. You're safe."

Her wide eyes met his. "Could I have that in writing, notarized, please?"

"If you like. But my word is usually considered equally binding," he replied. His hand fell and caught hers. "As for the multimillionaire bit, that's past history. I'm just an ordinary guy working his way up the corporate ladder right now. Come in and meet my guests.''

His fingers were warm and strong and she felt a rush of emotion that burst like tangible joy inside her. What was happening to her? As if he sensed her confusion and uncertainty, his fingers linked into hers and pressed reassuringly. Involuntarily her own returned the pressure.

As they gained the top of the steps, a vivacious brunette about Janine's age came up to them with a champagne glass in her hand. She beamed at Canton until she saw him holding hands with the other woman. Her smile became catty.

''There you are, Canton. I don't believe I know your friend, do I?'' she asked pointedly, glancing at Janine.

''Probably not. Janine Curtis, this is Missy Elliger. She's the daughter of one of my oldest friends.''

''You're not that old, darling,'' she drawled, moving closer to him. She glared at Janine. ''Do you live here?''

''Oh, no,'' Janine said pleasantly. ''I live in a commune in California with several men.''

The other woman gaped at her.

''Behave,'' Canton said shortly, increasing the pressure of his fingers. ''This is Janine Curtis. She's here on vacation with her little brother. That's him, over there with Karie. His name's Kurt.''

''Oh.'' Missy cleared her throat. ''What a very odd thing to say, Miss…Curtsy?''

''Curtis.'' Janine corrected her easily. ''Why do you say it's odd?''

''Well, living in a commune. Really!''

Janine shrugged. ''Actually it wasn't so much a commune as it was a sort of, well, labor camp. You know, where they send political prisoners? I voiced unpopular thoughts about the government..."

"*In America?!*" Missy burst out.

"Heavens, no! In one of the Balkan countries. I seem to forget which one. Anyway, there I was, with my trusty rifle, shooting snipers with my platoon when the lights went out..."

"Platoon?"

"Not in this life, of course," Janine went on, unabashed. "I believe it was when I was a private in the Czech army."

Missy swallowed her champagne in one gulp. "I must speak to Harvey Winthrop over there. Do excuse me." She gave Canton a speaking look and escaped.

Canton was trying not to laugh.

Janine wiggled her eyebrows at him. "Not bad for a spur-of-the-moment story, huh?"

"You idiot!"

She smiled. He wasn't bad at all. His eyes twinkled even when he didn't smile back.

"I'm sorry," she said belatedly. "She's really got a case on you, you know."

"Yes, I do," he replied. He brought up their linked hands. "That's why I'm doing this."

All her illusions fell, shattered, at her feet. "Oh."

"Surely you didn't think there was any other reason?" he mused. "After all, we're almost a generation apart. In fact, you're only a year older than Missy is."

"So I'm a visual aid."

He chuckled, pressing her fingers. "In a sense. I didn't think you'd mind. Enemies do help one another on occasion. I'll do the same for you, one day."

"I'm not that much in demand," she said, feeling stiff and uncomfortable now that she understood his odd behavior. "But you can have anyone you like. I read it in a magazine article."

"Was that the story they ran next to the one about space aliens attending the latest White House dinner?" he asked politely.

She glowered up at him. "You know what I mean."

He shrugged. "I'm off women temporarily. My wife wrote me off as a failure and found someone richer," he added, with a lack of inflection that was more revealing than the cold emptiness in his eyes.

"More fool, her," she said with genuine feeling. "You'll make it all back and she'll be sorry."

He smiled, surprised. "No, she won't. The magic left during the second year of our marriage. We stayed together for Karie, but eventually we didn't even see each other for months at a time. It was a marriage on paper. She's happier with her new husband, and I'm happier alone." He stared out to sea. "The sticking point is Karie. We ended up with joint custody, and that doesn't suit her. She thinks Karie belongs with her."

"How does Karie feel?"

"Oh, she likes tagging along with me and going on business trips," he said. "She's learning things that she wouldn't in the exclusive girls' school Marie wants her in. I pulled her out of school and brought her here with me for a couple of weeks, mainly to get her out of reach of Marie. She's made some veiled threats lately about wanting more alimony or full custody."

"Education is important."

He glared at her. "And Karie will get the necessary education. She's only missing a few weeks of school and she's so intelligent that she'll catch up in no time.

But I want her to have more than a degree and a swelled head when she grows up.''

She felt insulted. ''You don't like academics?''

He shrugged. ''I've been put down by too damned many of them, while they tried to copy my software,'' he countered. ''I like to design it. But in the past, I spent too much time at a computer and too little with my daughter. Even if I hadn't lost everything, taking a break was long overdue.''

''You went to Silicon Valley, Karie said.''

''Yes. Among other reasons, I was looking for guinea pigs.'' He glanced down at her with a faint scowl. ''Come to think of it, there's you.''

''Me?''

''I need someone to test a new program for me,'' he continued surprisingly. ''It's a variation on one of my first word processors, but this one has a new configuration that's more efficient. It's still in the development stages, but it's usable. What do you think?''

She wasn't sure. She'd lost whole chapters before to new software and she was working on a deadline.

''Don't worry about it right now,'' he said. ''Think it over and let me know.''

''Okay. It's just that… Well, my boss wants this project sent up within a month. I can't really afford to change software in the middle of it.''

''No, you can't. And I didn't mean I wanted you to download the program within the next ten minutes,'' he added dryly.

''Oh. Well, in that case, yes, I'll think about it.''

His hand tightened over hers. ''Good.''

He led her through his guests, making introductions. Surprisingly his friends came from all walks of life and most of them were ordinary people. A few were very wealthy, but they didn't act superior or out of order at all. However, Missy Elliger watched Janine with narrow, angry eyes and faint contempt.

"Your guest over there looks as if she'd like to plant that glass she's holding in the middle of my forehead," she commented as they were briefly alone.

"Missy likes a challenge. She's too young for me."

She glanced at him. "So you said."

His eyes searched hers. "And I'm not in the market for a second Mrs. Rourke."

"Point taken," she said.

His eyebrow jerked. "No argument?"

Her eyes sparkled. "I wasn't aware that I'd proposed to you," she replied with a grin. "We're temporary neighbors and frequent sparring partners. That's all."

"What if I'd like to be more than your neighbor?" he asked with deliberate sensuality.

Her grin didn't waver. That was amusement in his face, not real interest. He was mocking her, and he wasn't going to get away with it. "Quentin might get upset about that."

"Quentin? Is there a real husband somewhere in the background?" he probed.

She hesitated. He hadn't bought the commune story, so there was no way he was going to buy a secret husband. This man was a little too savvy for her usual ways of dissuading pursuers.

"A male friend," she countered with a totally straight face.

The hand holding hers let go, gently and unobtrusively, but definitely. "You didn't mention him before."

"There wasn't really an opportunity to," she countered. She smiled up at him. "He's a college professor. He teaches medieval history at the University of Indiana on the Chicago campus, where my parents teach anthropology."

His stance seemed to change imperceptibly. "Your parents are college professors?"

"Yes. They're on a dig in some Mayan ruins in Quintana Roo. Kurt's been ill with tonsillitis and complications. They took him out of school to get completely well and I'm tutoring him with his lessons until he goes back. We're near our parents, here in this villa, and I can get some work done and take care of Kurt as well."

He was wary, now, and not at all amused. "I suppose you have a degree, too?" he continued.

She wondered about the way he was looking at her, at the antagonistic set of his head, but she let it go by and took the question at face value. "Well, yes. I have an honors baccalaureate degree in history with a minor in German."

He seemed to withdraw without even moving. He set his glass on an empty tray and his lean hands slid into his pockets. His eyes moved restlessly around the room.

"What sort of degree do you have?" she asked.

It was the wrong question. He closed up completely. "Let me introduce you to the Moores," he said, taking her elbow. "They're interesting people."

She felt the new coolness in his manner with a sense of loss. She'd either offended him or alienated him. Perhaps he had some deep-seated prejudices about archaeology, which was the branch of anthropology in which both her parents specialized. She was about to tell him that they were both active in helping to enact legislation to help protect burial sites and insure that human skeletal remains were treated with dignity and respect.

But he was already making the introductions, to a nice young couple in real estate. A minute later, he excused himself and went pointedly to join his friend Missy Elliger, whom he'd said was too young for him. Judging by the way he latched onto her hand, and held it, he'd already forgotten that she was too young for him. Or, she mused humorously, he'd decided that Missy was less dangerous than Janine. How very flattering!

But the rest of the evening was a dead loss as far as Janine was concerned. She felt ill at ease and somewhat contagious, because he made a point of keeping out of her way. He was very polite, and courteous, but he might as well have been on another planet. It was such a radical and abrupt shift that it puzzled her.

Even Karie and Kurt noticed, from their vantage point beside a large potted palm near the patio.

"They looked pretty good together for a few minutes," Kurt said.

"Yes," she agreed, balancing a plate of cake on her knee. "Then they seemed to explode apart, didn't they?"

"Janie doesn't like men to get too close," Kurt told her with a grimace. "The only reason her boyfriend, Quentin, has lasted so long is because he forgets her for weeks at a time when he's translating old manuscripts."

"He what?" Karie asked, her fork poised in midair.

"He forgets her," he replied patiently. "And since he isn't pushy and doesn't try to get her to marry him, they get along just fine. Janine likes her independence," he added. "She doesn't want to get married."

"I guess my dad feels that way right now, too," Karie had to admit. "But he and my mom were never together much. Mom hates him now because she couldn't get exclusive custody of me. She swore she'd get me away from him eventually, but we haven't heard from her in several weeks. I suppose she's forgotten. He's forgetful, too, sometimes, when he's working on some new program. I guess that's hard on moms."

"He and Janie would make the perfect couple," Kurt ventured. "They'd both be working on something new all the time."

"But it doesn't look like they'll be thinking about it now," Karie said sadly. "See how he's holding Missy's hand?"

"He was holding Janie's earlier," Kurt reminded her.

"Yes, but now they're all dignified and avoiding each other." She sighed. "Grown-ups! Why do they have to make everything so complicated?"

"Beats me. Here. Have some more cake."

"Thanks!" She took a big bite. "Maybe they could use a helping hand. You know. About getting comfortable with each other."

"I was just thinking that myself," Kurt said. He grinned at his partner in crime. "Got any ideas?"

"I'm working on some."

Meanwhile, oblivious to the fact that she was soon going to become a guinea pig in quite another way than software testing, Janine sat in a corner with a couple whose passion was deep-sea fishing and spent the next hour being bored out of her mind.

Chapter Four

"Never, never get me roped into another party at the Rourkes'," Janine told her brother the next morning. "I'd rather be shot than go back there."

"Karie said she went home with her parents, after the party," Kurt said cautiously.

She pretended oblivion. "She, who?"

"Missy Elliger," he prompted. "You know, the lady who had Mr. Rourke by the hand all night?"

"She could have had him by the nose, for all I care," she said haughtily, and without meaning a word of it.

He glanced at her, and smiled secretively, but he didn't say anything.

"I think I'll invite Quentin down for the weekend," she said after a minute.

His eyebrows were vocal. "Why?"

She didn't want to admit why. "Why not?" she countered belligerently.

He shrugged. "Suit yourself."

"I know you don't like him, but he's really very nice when you get to know him."

"He's okay. I just hate ancient history. We have to study that stuff in school."

"What they're required to teach you usually is boring," she said. "And notice that I said 'required to.' Teachers have to abide by rules and use the textbooks they're assigned. In college, it's different. You get to hear about the *real* people. That includes all the naughty bits." She grinned. "You'll love it."

He sighed irritably. "No, I won't."

"Give Quentin a chance," she pleaded.

"If you like him, I guess he's okay. It just seems like he's always trying to change you into somebody else." He studied her through narrowed eyes. "Are you sure you don't like Karie's dad?"

She cringed inside, remembering how receptive she'd been last night to his pretended advances, before she knew they were pretend. She'd tingled at the touch of his hand, and he probably knew it, too. She felt like an idiot for letting her emotions go like that, for letting them show, when he was only using her to keep Missy at bay. And why had he bothered, when he spent the rest of the night holding the awful woman's hand?

"Yes, I'm sure," she lied glibly. "Now let me get to work."

"Will Quentin stay here?" he asked before he left her.

"Why not?" she asked. "You can be our chaperon."

He sighed. "Mom and Dad won't like it."

"I'm old enough, and Quentin probably wants to marry me," she said. "He just doesn't know it yet."

"You wouldn't marry him!" he exclaimed.

She shifted. "Why not? I'm going on twenty-five. I should get married. I want to get married. Quentin is steady and loyal and intelligent."

Also the wrong sort of man for Janine to get serious about, Kurt thought, but he held his tongue. This wasn't a good idea to get his sister more upset than she already was. Besides, he was thinking, having Quentin here just might make Karie's dad a little jealous. There were all sorts of possibilities that became more exciting by the minute. He smiled secretively and waved as he left her to her computer.

"Janie's boyfriend is coming to stay," he told Karie later, making sure he spoke loudly enough that her father, who was sitting just down the beach, heard him.

"Her boyfriend?" Karie asked, shocked. "You mean, she has a boyfriend?"

"Oh, yes, she does," he said irritably, plopping down beside her in the sand. "He teaches ancient history. He's brainy and sophisticated and crazy about her."

Karie made a face. "I thought you said she wasn't interested in getting married."

"She said this morning that she was," he replied. "It would be just my luck to end up with him as my brother-in-law."

Karie giggled at the concept. "Is he old?"

"Sure," he said gloomily. "At least thirty-five."

"That's old," she agreed.

Down the beach, a young-thinking man of thirty-eight glared in their general direction. Thirty-five wasn't old. And what the hell was Janine thinking to saddle herself with an academic? He wanted to throw something. She had a degree, he reminded himself. Her parents were academics; even her boyfriend was.

But Canton Rourke was a high-school dropout with a certificate that said he'd passed a course giving him the equivalent of a high-school diploma. He'd been far too busy making money to go to college. Now, it was too late. He couldn't compete with an educated woman on her level.

But he was attracted to her. That was the hell of it. He didn't want to be. Freshly divorced, awash in a sea of financial troubles, he had no room in his life for a new woman. Especially a young and pretty and very intelligent woman like Janine. He'd been smitten before, but never this fast or this furiously. He didn't know what he was going to do.

Except that he was sure he didn't want the college professor to walk away with his neighbor.

Janine called Quentin later that day. "Why don't you fly down here for a couple of days," she suggested.

"I can't leave in the middle of the summer semester, with classes every day," he replied. "I've got students who have makeup exams to take, too."

She sighed. "Quentin, you could leave early Friday and fly back Sunday."

"That's a rather large expense for two days' holiday," he replied thoughtfully.

She felt her temper oozing over its dam. "Well, you're right about that," she agreed hotly, "my company is hardly worth the price of an airline ticket."

"Wh…what?"

"Never mind. Have a nice summer, Quentin." She hung up.

Kurt stuck his head around the door. "Is he coming?"

She glared at him and threw a sofa pillow in his general direction.

Kurt went out the patio door, whistling to himself.

Janine sank into the depths of depression for the next hour. She and Quentin were good friends, and in the past few months, they'd gone out a lot together socially. But to give him credit, he'd never mentioned marriage or even a serious relationship. A few light, careless kisses didn't add up to a proposal of marriage. She was living in pipe dreams again, and she had to stop.

But this was the worst possible time to discover that she didn't have a steady boyfriend, when she wanted to prove to Canton Rourke that he had no place at all in her life. As if she'd want a washed-up ex-millionaire, right?

Wrong. She found him so attractive that her toes curled every time she thought about him. He was the stuff of which dreams were made, and not because he'd been fabulously wealthy, either. It was the man himself, not his empire, that appealed to Janine. She wondered if he'd believe that? He was probably so used to people trying to get close to his wallet that he never knew if they liked him for himself.

But she didn't want him to know that she did. If only Quentin hadn't been so unreasonable! Why couldn't he simply walk out on his classes, risk being fired and spend his savings to rush down here to Cancún and save Janine's pride from the rejection of a man she coveted?

She burst out laughing. Putting things back into perspective did have an effect, all right.

The phone rang. She picked up the receiver.

"Janie?" Quentin murmured. "I've reconsidered. I think I'd like to come down for the weekend. I can get Professor Mills to take my Friday classes. I need a break."

She grinned into the telephone. "That would be lovely, Quentin!"

"But I'll have to leave on Sunday," he added firmly. "I've got to prepare for an exam."

"A few days will be nice. You'll like it here."

"I'll pack plenty of bottled water."

"You won't need to," she told him. "We have plenty. And at the restaurants, we've never had a problem."

"All right then. I'll phone you from the airport when I get in. I'll try to leave early in the morning, if there's a flight. I'll phone you."

"Bring your bathing trunks."

There was a pause. "Janine, I don't swim."

She sighed. "I forgot."

"Where are your parents?"

"Still out at the dig."

"You'd better book me in at a nearby hotel," he said.

"You could stay with Kurt and me..."

"Not wise, Janine," he murmured indulgently. "We aren't that sort of people, and I have a position to consider. You really must think more conventionally, if we're to have any sort of future together."

It was the first time he'd mentioned having a future with her. And suddenly, she didn't want to think about it.

"I understand that the Spaniards landed near Cancún, on Cozumel," he said. "I'd love to take the time to search through the local library, if they're open on Saturday. I read Spanish, you know."

She did know. He never missed an opportunity to remind her. Of course, he also spoke Latin, French, German and a little Russian. He was brilliant. That was what had attracted her to him at first. Now, she wondered what in the world had possessed her to ask him down here. He'd go off on an exploration of Spanish history in the New World and she wouldn't see him until he was ready to fly out. On the other hand, that might not be so bad.

"I'll meet you at the airport."

"Good! See you Friday. And Janine, this time, try not to forget to take the car keys out of the ignition before you lock the door, hmmm?"

She broke the connection and stared out the window. What in heaven's name had she done? Quentin's favorite pastime was putting her down. In the time since she'd seen him, she'd forgotten. But now she remembered with painful clarity why she'd been happy to leave Bloomington, Indiana, behind just a few months ago and move to a small apartment in Chicago. How could she have forgotten?

Later in the day, she noticed again the dark man who'd been watching Karie on the beach. He was downtown when she took the kids in a cab to visit one of the old cathedrals there, for research on the book she was writing.

He didn't come close or speak to them, but he watched their movements very carefully. He had a cellular phone, too, which he tried to conceal before Janine spotted it. She went toward a nearby policeman, intent on asking him to question the man. About that time, her intentions were telegraphed to the watchful dark man, and he immediately got into a car and left the area. It disturbed Janine, and she wondered whether or not she should tell Canton about it. She didn't mention it to Karie or Kurt. After all, it could have been perfectly innocent. There was no sense in upsetting everyone without good reason.

They arrived back at the beach house tired and sweaty. The heat was making everyone miserable. Here, at least, there was a constant wind coming off the ocean. She made lemonade for the three of them and they were sitting on the patio, drinking it, when Canton came strolling along the beach below them.

He was wearing dark glasses and an angry expression. He came up onto the deck two steps at a time. When he reached the top, he whipped off the dark glasses and glared at his daughter.

"When I got back from Tulsa, the house was empty and there was no note," he said. "Your lack of consideration is wearing a little thin. Do I have to forbid you to leave the house to get some cooperation?"

Karie groaned. "Dad, I'm sorry!" she exclaimed, jumping up out of her chair. "Kurt and Janie asked me to go to town with them on a re—"

"Recreational trip," Janine added at once, to forestall her young guest from using "research trip" and spilling the beans about her alter ego.

"Recreational trip," Karie parroted obediently. "I was so excited that I just forgot about the note. Don't be mad."

"I've lost half a day worrying where you were," he said shortly. "I've phoned everyone we know here, including the police."

"You can take away my allowance for three years. Six," she added helpfully. "I'll give up chocolate cake forever."

"You hate chocolate," he murmured irritably.

"Yes, but for you, I'll stop eating it."

He chuckled reluctantly. "Go home. And next time you don't leave me a note, you're grounded for life."

"Yes, sir! See you, Janie and Kurt. Thanks for the trip!"

"I have to wash my pet eel," Kurt said at once with a grin at Janie, and got out of the line of fire.

"Craven coward," she muttered after him.

"Strategic retreat," Canton observed with narrowed eyes. He looked down at her. "You're corrupting my daughter."

"I'm what?"

"Corrupting her. She never used to be this irresponsible." His eyes grew cold. "And if you're going to have your boyfriend living here with you, without a chaperon, she isn't coming near the place until he leaves!"

She actually gaped at him. "Exactly what century are you living in?" she exclaimed.

"That's your boyfriend's specialty, I believe, ancient history," he continued. "I've seen too many permissive life-styles to have any respect for them. I won't have my daughter exposed to yours!"

"Permissive...exposed..." She was opening and closing her mouth like a fish. "You're one to talk, with your hot and cold running women and your...your cover girl lovers!"

"Escorts," he said shortly. "I was never unfaithful to my wife. Which is a statement she damned sure couldn't make! I'm not raising Karie to be like her."

She felt pale and wondered if she looked it. Her hands were curled painfully into the arms of her chair. She'd never been verbally attacked with such menace. "My boyfriend is a respected college professor with a sterling moral character," she said finally. "And for your information, he insists on staying in a hotel, not here!"

He stood there, towering over her, hands deep in his pockets, barely breathing as his blue eyes went over her light cotton dress down to the splayed edges of her skirt that revealed too much of her lovely, tanned long legs.

She tossed the skirt back over them and sat up, furious. "But even if he did decide to stay here, it would be none of your business!" She got to her feet, glaring up at him. "You can keep Karie at home if you're afraid of my corrupting influence. And you can stay away, too, damn you!"

The speed with which his lean hands came out of his pockets to catch her bare arms was staggering. He whipped her against the length of him and stared down into shocked, wide green eyes.

"Damn you, too," he said under his breath, searching her face with an intensity that almost hurt. "You're too young, too flighty, too emotional, too everything! I'm sorry I ever brought Karie down here!"

"So am I!" she raged. "Let me go!" She kicked out at his leg with her bare foot.

The action, far too violent to be controlled, caused her to lose her balance, and brought her into a position so intimate that she trembled helplessly at the contact.

His hands were on her back now, preventing a fall, slowly moving, sensuous. "Careful," he said, and his voice was so sensual that she lost all will to fight.

Her fingers clenched into the front of his knit shirt. She couldn't make herself look up. The feel of his body was overpowering enough, without the electric pull of those blue, blue eyes to make her even worse. She didn't move at all. She wasn't sure that she could. He smelled of spice and soap. She liked the clean scent of his body. In the opening of his shirt there was a thick mat of hair showing, and she wondered helplessly if it went all the way down to his slacks. She wondered how it would feel under her hands, her cheek, her mouth. Her thoughts shocked her.

His big hands splayed on her back, moving her closer. His breath at her temple stirred her short hair warmly.

His nose moved against her forehead, against her own nose, her cheek. His thin lips brushed her cheek and the corner of her mouth, pausing there as they had once before, teasing, taunting.

She felt her breath shaking out of her body against his lips, but she couldn't help it. His mouth was the only thing in the world. She stared at it with such hunger that nothing else existed.

His hand came up. His thumb brushed lightly against her lower lip, and then slightly harder, tugging. As her lips parted, his head bent. She felt the whispery pressure with a sense of trembling anticipation, with hungry curiosity.

"Close your eyes, for God's sake," he breathed as his mouth opened. "Not your mouth, though…"

She imagined the kiss. She could already feel it. It would be as unexpected as the sudden surge of the wind around them. She felt her body stiffen with the shock of desire it kindled in her. She'd never had such an immediate reaction to any man. He would be experienced, of course. His very demeanor told her that he knew everything there was to know about kissing. She was lost from the very first touch. Her eyes closed, as he'd told them to, and her mouth opened helplessly. She heard someone moan as she anticipated the heat and passion of his embrace...

"Do you know who I am?" he asked.

Her eyes opened. He hadn't moved. He hadn't kissed her. His mouth was still poised, waiting. She'd...imagined the kiss. Her eyes shot up, struggling to cope with steamy emotions that had her knees shaking.

His eyes held hers. "I'm not your college professor," he murmured. "Are you missing him so much that even I can stand in for him?" he added with a mocking smile.

She tore out of his arms with pure rage, her face red, her eyes and hair wild.

"Yes!" she cried at him. "I'm missing him just that much! That's why I invited him to come down to Cancún!"

His hands went back into his pockets, and he didn't even look ruffled. She was enraged.

His eyebrow jerked as he looked at her with kindling amusement, and something much darker. "You're still too young," he remarked. "But whatever effect your boyfriend has had on you is minimal at best."

"He has a wonderful effect on me!"

His eyelids dropped over twinkling eyes. "Like I just did?"

"That was...it was..."

He moved a little closer, his stance sensually threatening. "Sensuous," he breathed, watching her mouth. "Explosive. Passionate. And I didn't even kiss you."

Her hand came up in a flash, but he caught it in his and brought the damp palm to his mouth in a gesture that made her catch her breath. His eyes were intent, dangerous.

"We come from different worlds," he said quietly. "But something inside each of us knows the other. Don't deny it," he continued when she started to protest. "It's no use. You knew me the minute we met, and I knew you."

"Oh, sure, when I was a soldier in the Czech army in some other life...!"

The back of his fingers stopped the words, gently. "I'm not a great believer in reincarnation," he continued. "But we know each other at some level. All the arguments in the world can't disguise it."

"I don't want you!" she sputtered.

His fingers caught hers and held them almost comfortingly. "Well, I want you," he said shortly. "But you're perfectly safe with me. Even if you didn't have a boyfriend, you'd be safe. I don't want involvement."

"You said that already."

"I'm saying it again, just to make the point. We're neighbors. That's all."

"I know," she snapped. She moved away, and his hand let go. "Stop touching me."

"I'm trying to," he replied with an odd smile. "It's like giving up smoking."

"I don't like you to touch me," she lied.

He didn't even bother with a reply. "I wouldn't dare kiss you," he said. "Addictions are dangerous."

She expelled a shaky breath. "Exactly."

His pale eyes searched hers for a long moment, and

the world around them vanished for that space of seconds.

"When you've had a couple of serious affairs and I've remade my fortune, I'll come back around."

She glared at him. "I don't like rich people."

His eyebrows shot up. "I'm not rich and you don't like me."

"You're still rich inside," she muttered.

"And you're just a little college girl with a heartless boss," he murmured. He smiled. "You could come to work for me. I'd give you paid holidays."

"You don't have a business."

"Yet," he replied, smiling with such confidence that she believed in that instant that he could do anything he liked.

"But you will have," she added.

He nodded. "And I'll need good and loyal employees."

"How do you know I'd be one?"

"You're working on your vacation. How much more loyal could you be?"

She averted her eyes. "Maybe I'm not exactly what I seem."

"Yes, you are. You're the most refreshing female I've met in years," he confessed reluctantly. "You're honest and loyal and unassuming. God, I'm so tired of socialites and actresses and authoresses who attract attention with every move and can't live out of the limelight! It's a relief to meet a woman who's satisfied just to be a cog instead of the whole damned wheel!"

She felt a blush coming on. He had no idea what her normal life was like. She was a very famous authoress indeed, and on her way to a large bankroll. She wasn't a cog, she was a whole wheel, in her niche, and even reviewers liked her. But this man, if he knew the truth, would be very disillusioned. He'd lost so much because he'd trusted the wrong people. How would he feel if he knew that Janine had lied to him?

But that wouldn't really matter, because he didn't want an intimate relationship and neither did she.

"Well, as one neighbor to another, you're fairly refreshing yourself. I've never met a down-on-his-luck millionaire before."

He smiled faintly. "New experiences are good for us. Short of kissing you, that is. I'm not that brave."

"Good thing," she replied, tongue-in-cheek. "I don't know where you've been."

He smiled. He laughed. He chuckled. "Good God!"

"I don't," she emphasized. "You are who you kiss."

"Bull. Your mouth doesn't know one damned thing about kissing."

"Oh, yes, it does."

His chin lifted. "I might consider letting you prove that one day. Not today," he added. "I'm getting old. It isn't safe to have my blood pressure tried too much in one afternoon."

"Is it high?" she asked with real concern.

He shrugged. "It tends to be. But not dangerously so." He searched her eyes. "Don't care about me. You're the last complication I need."

"I was about to say the same thing. Besides, I have a boyfriend."

"Good luck to him," he replied with a short laugh. "If you're pristine at twenty-four, he's lacking something."

Her mouth opened without words, but he was already leaving the deck before the right sort of words presented themselves. And of all the foul names she could think of to call him, only "scoundrel" came immediately to mind.

"Schurke!" she yelled in German.

He didn't break stride. But he turned, smiled and winked at her. His smile took the wind right out of her sails.

While she was still trying to think up a comeback, he walked on down the beach and out of earshot. The man was a mystery—and what she felt when he was around her was a puzzle she was unsure she'd ever solve.

Chapter Five

For the next hour, Janine did her best to look forward to Quentin's forthcoming visit. She and Quentin were good friends, and in the past, while she was still living at home, they'd gone out a lot together socially. But to give him credit, he'd never mentioned marriage or even a serious relationship. A few light, careless kisses didn't add up to a proposal of marriage.

On the other hand, what she experienced with Canton Rourke was so explosive that all she could think about was the fact that one day soon, she'd have to go back to Chicago and never see him again. In a very short time, she'd come to know their down-on-his-luck neighbor in ways she never should have. She wanted him just as much as he wanted her, despite the fact that he infuriated her most of the time. But she was living in dreams again, and she had to stop. Having Quentin here even for a weekend might snap her out of her growing infatuation with Canton Rourke.

Quentin came down three days later. He got off the

plane in Cancún, looking sweaty and rumpled and thoroughly out of humor. He sent a dark glare at a young woman with red hair who smiled at him sweetly and then sent a kiss his way.

Quentin glared after the woman as he joined Janie, carry-on bag in hand. He wiped his sweaty light brown hair with his handkerchief, and his dark eyes weren't happy.

"English majors," he spat contemptuously. "They think they know everything!"

"Some of them do," Janine remarked. "One of my English professors spoke five languages and had a photographic memory."

"I had old Professor Blake, who couldn't remember where his car was parked from hour to hour."

"I know how he felt," she murmured absently as she scanned the airport for the rental car she was driving.

He groaned. "Janie, you didn't lock the keys in it?"

She produced them from her pocket and jangled them. "No, I didn't. I just can't remember where I put it. But it will come to me. Let's go. Did you have a nice flight?"

"No. The English professor sat beside me on the plane and contradicted every remark I made. What a boor!"

She bit her tongue trying not to remind him that he did the same thing to her, constantly.

"God, it's hot here! Is it any cooler at the hotel?"

"Not much," she said. "There's air-conditioning inside. It helps. And there's always a breeze on the beach."

"I want to find the library first thing," he said.

"And then the local historical society. I speak Spanish, so I'll be able to converse with them quite well."

"Do you speak Mayan?" she asked with a smile. "I do hope so, because quite a few people here speak Mayan instead of Spanish."

He looked so uncomfortable that she felt guilty.

"But most everyone knows some English," she added quickly. "You'll do fine."

"I hope that redheaded pit viper isn't staying at my hotel. Where is my hotel, by the way?" he demanded.

"It's about three miles from my beach house, in the hotel zone. I can drive you to and from, though. I rented the car for a month."

"Isn't it dangerous to drive here?"

"Not any more dangerous than it is to drive in Chicago," she replied. "Ah. There it is!"

"I thought your brother was with you," he remarked.

"He is. He has a playmate, and he's staying with her family today." She didn't add that he'd refused to go to meet Quentin, who wasn't one of his favorite people.

"I see. Is he still as outspoken and ill-mannered as ever?"

She hated that smug smile of his. This was going to be a fiasco of a vacation, she could see it right now.

Kurt was polite to Quentin; just polite and no more. He spent the weekend tagging after Karie and avoiding the beach house where Quentin was poring over copies of old manuscripts he'd found in some archives. They were all in Spanish. Old Spanish.

"This is sixteenth century," he murmured absently, with pages spread all over the sofa and the floor while he sat cross-legged on the small rug going from one to another. "Some of these verbs I don't even recognize. They may be archaic, of course…"

He was talking to himself. Across from him, Janine was poring over a volume on forensic medicine, searching for new methods of bumping off her villains.

Into the middle of their studious afternoon, Karie and Kurt came back from a walk on the beach, with Karie's father looming menacingly behind them. Both children were flushed and guilty-looking.

Janine laid her volume aside and sighed. "What have you done, now?" she asked Kurt with resignation.

"Remember the garden hose I bought them?" Canton asked her with barely a glance for the disorderly papers and man on the floor.

"Yes," Janine said slowly.

"They were hacking it up with a very sharp machete under the porch at our place."

"A machete? Where did you get a machete?" Janine exclaimed to Kurt.

Before he could answer, Quentin got to his feet, his gold-rimmed glasses pushed down on his nose for reading. "I told you that you'd never be able to handle Kurt by yourself," Quentin said helpfully.

Janine glared at him. "I don't 'handle' Kurt. He's not an object, Quentin."

Canton had his hands deep in his pockets. He was looking at Quentin with curiosity and faint contempt.

"This is our neighbor, Mr. Rourke," Janine introduced. "And this is Quentin Hobard, a colleague of my parents' from Bloomington, Indiana. He teaches ancient history at Indiana University."

"How ancient?" Canton asked.

"Renaissance," came the reply. He held up a photocopied page of spidery Spanish script. "I'm researching—"

Midsentence, Canton took the page from him and gave it a cursory, scowling scrutiny. "It's from a diary. Much like the one Bernal Díaz kept when he first came from Spain to the New World with Cortés and began protesting the *encomienda*."

Quentin was impressed. "Why, yes!"

"But this writing deals with the Mayan, not the Aztec, people." Canton read the page aloud, effortlessly translating the words into English.

Rourke finally looked up. "Who wrote this?" he asked.

Quentin blinked. He, like the others, had been listening spellbound to the ancient words spoken so eloquently by their visitor.

"No one knows," the scholar replied. "They're recorded as anonymous, but he writes as if he were a priest, doesn't he? How did you read it?" he added. "Some of those verbs are obsolete."

"My mother was Spanish," Rourke replied. "She came from Valladolid and spoke a dialect that passed down almost unchanged from the Reconquista."

"Yes, when Isabella and Ferdinand united their kingdoms through marriage and drove the Moors from Spain, in 1492. They were married in Valladolid," Quentin added. "Have you been there?"

"Yes," Rourke replied. "I still have cousins in Valladolid."

This was fascinating. Janine stared at him with open curiosity, met his glittery gaze and blushed.

"Well, thank you for the translation," Quentin said.

"I'd be very interested to have you do some of the other pages if you have time."

"Sorry," Rourke replied, "but I have to fly to New York in the morning. I should be back by midnight. I wanted to ask Janie if she'd keep my daughter while I'm away."

It was the first time he'd abbreviated her name. She felt all thumbs, and was practically tongue-tied. "Why...of course," she stammered. "I'd be glad to."

"I'll send her over before I leave. It'll be early."

"Good luck getting a flight out," Quentin murmured.

Canton chuckled. "No problem there. I have a Lear-jet. See you in the morning, then." He glanced down at the book lying on the sofa and his eyebrows went up. "Forensic medicine? I thought history was your field."

"It is," Janine said.

"Oh, she does that for her books," Quentin said offhandedly.

"The ones I'm trying to sell," she added quickly, with a glare at Quentin.

He didn't understand. He started to speak, but Janine got to her feet and walked Canton to the door.

"I took the machete away from them, by the way, and hid it." He glanced past her at the kids, who were on the patio by now. "Don't let them out of your sight. Good God, I don't know what's gotten into them. Why would they hack up a perfectly good garden hose?"

"Fishing bait to catch gardeners?" she suggested.

He made a gruff sound. Behind her, Quentin was already reading again, apparently having forgotten that he wasn't alone.

"Dedicated, isn't he?" he murmured.

"He loves his subject. I love it, too, but my period is Victorian America. I don't really care much for earlier stuff."

He searched her eyes. "Do tell?"

"You're very well educated," she remarked. "You read Spanish like a native."

"I am a native, as near as not, even if I don't look it," he replied. He lifted his chin. "As for the education part, I was a little too busy in my youth to get past the tenth grade. I have a certificate that gives me the equivalent of a high-school diploma. That's all."

She went scarlet. She'd had no idea that he wasn't college educated. He'd been a millionaire, and had all the advantages. Or had he?

The blush fascinated him. He touched it. "So you see, I'm not an academic at all. Far from it, in fact. I got my education on the streets."

Her eyes met his. "No one who could invent the software you've come up with is ignorant. You're a genius in your own right."

His intake of breath was audible. He looked odd for a moment, as if her remark had taken him off guard.

"Weren't your parents well-off?" she asked.

"You mean, did I inherit the money that got me started? No, I didn't," he replied. "I made every penny myself. Actually, Miss Enigma, my father was a laborer. I had to drop out of school to support my sister when he died of cancer. I was seventeen. My mother had already died when I was fourteen."

She did gasp, this time. "And you got that far, alone?"

"Not completely alone, but I made every penny honestly." He chuckled. "I'm a workaholic. Doesn't it show?"

She nodded. "The intelligence shows, too."

He cocked an eyebrow and there was an unpleasant smile on his firm mouth. "Buttering me up, in case I make it all back?"

She glowered. "Do I look as if money matters to me?"

"Women are devious," he replied. "You could look like an angel and still be mercenary."

Her pride was stung. "Thanks for the compliment." She turned to go back in.

He caught her arm, pulled her outside and shut the door. "Your pet scholar in there is an academic," he said through his teeth. "That's why you keep him around, isn't it? And I don't even have a high-school diploma."

"What does that matter?" she said with equal venom. "Who cares if you've got a degree? I don't! We're just neighbors for the summer," she added mockingly. "Just good friends."

His eyes fell to her mouth. "I'd like to be more," he said quietly.

The wind was blowing off the ocean. She felt it ruffle her hair. Sand whipped around her legs. She had no sense of time as she looked at his face and wondered about the man hidden behind it, the private one that he kept secret from the world.

Suddenly, with a muffled curse, he bent and brushed his lips lightly over hers, so softly that she wasn't sure he'd really done it.

"Thanks for looking after Karie," he said. "I'll pay you back."

"It's no hardship."

"Like children, don't you?" he murmured.

She smiled. "A lot."

"I love my daughter. I'd like a son, too." His gaze lifted to meet hers and he saw the pupils dilate suddenly. His jaw tautened. "Don't sleep with him," he said harshly, jerking his head toward the door.

Her jaw fell. "Sleep...!"

"Not with him, or anyone else." He bent again. This time the kiss was hard, brief, demanding, possessive. His eyes were glittering. "God, I wish I'd never met you," he said under his breath. And without another word, he turned and left her at the door, windblown and stunned, wondering what she'd done to make him kiss her—and then suddenly get angry all over again. She could still feel the pressure of his mouth long after she went back into the living room and tried to act normally.

Karie was a joy to have around, but she and Kurt seemed to find new ways to irritate Quentin all the time. From playing loud music when he was studying his manuscripts to refusing to leave Janine alone with him, they were utter pests.

And there was one more silent complication. The man was back again. He didn't come near the house, but Janine spotted his car along the highway most mornings. He just sat there, watching, the sun glinting off his binoculars. Once again, she started toward the road, and the car sped away. She was really getting nervous. And she hadn't heard from her parents.

She tried to explain her worries to Quentin, but he'd found a reference to Chichén Itzá in the manuscript and was dying to go there.

"There's a bus trip out to the ruins, but it takes all day, and you'll be very late getting back."

"That doesn't matter!" he exclaimed. "I have Saturday free. Come on, we'll both go."

"I can't take Kurt on a trip like that. He's still recovering."

He glared at her. "I can't miss this. It's the opportunity of a lifetime. There are glyphs on the temple that I really want to see."

She smiled. "Then go ahead. You'll have a good time."

He pursed his lips and nodded. "Yes, I will. You don't mind, do you?"

"Oh, of course not," she said. "Go ahead."

He smiled. "Thanks, Janine, I knew you'd be understanding about it."

When was she ever anything else, she wondered. He didn't mind leaving her behind, when they were supposed to be spending their vacation together. But, then, that was Quentin, thoughtless and determined to have his own way. She thought that she'd never forget the sound of Canton Rourke's deep voice as he translated that elegant Spanish into English. Quentin had been impressed, which was also unusual.

"Your neighbor looked very familiar, didn't he?" Quentin asked suddenly.

She had to fight down a thrill at just the mention of him. "He should. Haven't you looked at a newspaper recently? Canton Rourke? Founder of Chipgrafix software?"

"Good Lord!"

"That was him," she said.

"Imagine, a mind like that," Quentin mused. "He doesn't look all that important, does he? I would have passed him on the street without a second glance. But he still reminds me of somebody... Aha! I've got it! The alien on that science fiction series..."

"No," she said, shaking her head. "He doesn't really look much like him at all, once you've been around him for a while."

"Sounds like him, though," he countered. "Nice voice."

He wasn't supposed to like Canton Rourke. He was supposed to be jealous and icy and contemptuous of the man. She sighed. Nothing was going according to plan. Nothing at all.

Karie spent the next day with Janine while Quentin boarded a tour bus at his hotel and was gone all day and most of the night. He came over the next afternoon by cab, on his way to the airport.

"I had a great time at Chichén Itzá," he told Janine. "Of course, the English whiz was on the tour, too," he added sourly. "She's from Indianapolis and is going back on the same flight I am. I hope they seat her on the wing. She knows all about the Maya culture. Speaks Spanish fluently," he added with pure disgust. "Has a double major in English and archaeology. Show-off."

She didn't quite look at him. "Is she married?"

"Who'd have her?" he spat. "She's so smug. Read the stelae to me before the tour guide could."

She smothered a grin. "Imagine that."

"Yes." He still looked disgusted. "Well, it's been a wonderful trip, Janine. I'm glad you talked me into it. I've got some great things to take back to my classes, including several rolls of film at Chichén Itzá that I'll share with the archaeology department. Think your parents might like some shots?"

She hesitated to mention that they'd taken more slides of the site than most tourists ever would. "You might mention it to them," she said tactfully.

"I'll do that. Well, I'll see you when you come home to visit your parents, I suppose. Any word on how your parents are coming along at that new site?"

She shook her head. "I'm getting a little worried. I haven't heard anything in a couple of weeks, not even one piece of E-mail."

"Hard to find electrical outlets in the jungle, I imagine," he said and then grinned at his joke.

She didn't smile. "They have an emergency generator and a satellite hookup for their computers."

"Well, they'll turn up," he said airily, ignoring her obvious concern. "I have to rush or I'll miss my flight. Good to have seen you. You were right, Janine. I did need a break."

He brushed a careless kiss against her cheek and went back out to his waiting cab.

And that was that.

Janine was halfheartedly reading a tome on forensics while Kurt and Karie had gone out to the beach to watch a boy go up on a parasail, which she'd forbidden them to go near. The abrupt knock at the patio wall caught her attention. Her heart jumped when she found Karie's dad standing there, dressed in lightweight white slacks and a tan knit shirt that showed anyone who cared to look just how powerful the muscles in his chest and arms were. For a man his age, he was really tremendously fit.

"I'm looking for Karie," he said without greeting.

She was still stung from his cold words while Quentin had been poring over his photocopies. "They're down the beach watching a parasail go up. Don't worry, I told them not to go near the thing.''

He went to the railing, shaded his eyes and stared down the beach. "Okay, I see them. They're wading in the surf, watching."

"Oh."

He turned back to her and searched her flushed face quietly. "Where's the boyfriend?"

"Gone back to Indiana. You just missed him."

"Pity," he said languidly.

She laughed mirthlessly. "Right."

He glanced at her computer screen. A word processor had been pulled up, but no files were open. "That's obsolete," he stated. "Why aren't you using the new one?"

"Because it takes me forever to learn one." She smiled at him. "I guess they're all child's play to you. I couldn't write a computer program if my life depended on it!"

That was interesting. "Why not?"

"Because I can't do math," she said simply. "And I don't understand machines, either. You must have a natural gift for computer science."

He felt less inferior. "Something like that, maybe."

"You didn't go to school at all to learn how to write programs?"

He shook his head. "I worked with two men who were old NASA employees. They learned about computing in the space program. I suppose I picked up a lot from them. We started the company together. I bought them out eventually and kept going on my own."

"Then you must have known how to get the best and brightest people to work for you, and keep them."

He smiled faintly. "You aren't quite what I expected," he said unexpectedly.

"Excuse me?"

"Some academics use their education to make people who don't have one feel insignificant," he explained.

She smiled ruefully. "Oh, that would be a good trick, making a millionaire feel insignificant because I have a degree in history."

"What do you do with it?" he asked unexpectedly.

She stared at him. "Do with it?"

"Yes. Do you teach, like your parents?"

"No."

"Why not? Are you happy being a secretary and working for a slave driver?"

She remembered, belatedly, the fictional life she'd concocted. "Oh. Well, no, I don't, really. But degrees are a dime a dozen these days. I know a man with a doctorate in philosophy who's working at a fast-food joint back home. It was the only job he could get."

He leaned against the wall, with his hands in his pockets. "How fast do you type?"

"A little over a hundred words a minute."

He whistled. "Pretty good."

"Thanks."

"If I can get the refinancing I need, you can come to work for me," he suggested.

Was he trying to make up for his behavior when he'd said he was sorry he'd ever met her? She wondered. "That's a nice offer," she said.

"Think about it, then." He shouldered away from the wall. "I'll go get Karie and tell her I'm back."

"They won't have gone far. Have you found out

anything about that man who was watching her?" she added, concerned.

He scowled. "No."

"I guess that's good."

"I wouldn't say that," he said absently. His eyes met hers. "Has he turned up again?"

She sighed. "He's been around. He bothers me."

"I know. I'll keep digging and see what I discover."

She was staring at the computer, sitting there like a one-eyed predator, staring at her with its word processing program open and waiting.

"Busy?" he asked.

"I should be."

He held out a hand. "Come along with me to get Karie. Your work will still be there when you get back."

She smiled, tempted. This was going to be disastrous, but why not? It was just a walk, after all.

She turned off the computer and, hesitantly, took the hand he offered. It closed, warm and firm, around hers.

"I'm safe," he said when she flushed a little. "We'll hold hands, like two old friends, and pretend that we've known each other for twenty years."

"I'd have been four years old..."

His hand contracted. "I'm thirty-eight," he said. "You don't have to emphasize that fourteen-year jump I've got on you. I'm already aware of it."

"I was kidding."

"I'm not laughing." He didn't look at her. His eyes were on the beach as they descended the steps and walked along, above the damp sand.

Kurt gave them a curious look when he saw them

holding hands. He waved, grinned and went back to chasing down sand crabs and shells, the parasail already forgotten. Karie was much further down the beach, talking to some girls who were about her age. She hadn't looked their way yet.

"When are your parents due back?" he asked.

"God knows," she replied wearily. "They get involved and forget time altogether. They're like two children sometimes. Kurt and I have to keep a close eye on them, to keep them out of trouble. This time, we're a little worried about pothunters, too."

"Pothunters? Collectors, you mean?"

"Actually I mean the go-betweens, the people who steal archaeological treasures to sell on the black market. Sometimes they already have a buyer lined up. This is a brand-new site and my parents think it's going to be a major one in the Mayan category. If it's a rich dig, you can bet that they'll be in trouble. The government can't afford the sort of protection they'll need, either. I just hope they're watching their backs."

"They should be here, watching the two of you," he murmured.

"Not them," she said on a chuckle. "It's been an interesting upbringing. When I was twelve, I sort of became the oldest person in my family. I've taken care of Kurt, and them, since then."

His fingers eased between hers sensuously. "You should marry and have children of your own."

Her heart leapt. She'd never thought of that in any real sense until right now. She felt the strength and attraction of the man beside her and thought how wonderful it would be to have a child with him.

Her thoughts shocked her. Her hand jerked in his. He stopped walking and looked down at her. His eyes searched hers in the silence of the beach, unbroken except for the watery crash of the surf just a few feet away.

The sensations that ripped through her body were of a sort she'd never felt with anyone. It was electric, fascinating, complex and disturbing. They seemed to talk to each other in that space of seconds without saying a word.

Involuntarily she moved a step closer to him, so that she could feel the heat of his body and inhale the clean scent of it.

He let go of her hand and caught her gently by the shoulders. "Fourteen years," he reminded her gently. "And I'm a poor man right now."

She smiled gently. "I've always been on the cutting edge of poor," she said simply. "Money is how you keep score. It isn't why you do a job."

"Amazing."

"What is?"

"That's how I've always thought of it."

Her eyes traced his strong face quietly. "This isn't a good idea, is it?"

"No," he agreed honestly. "I'm vulnerable, and so are you. We're both out of our natural element, two strangers thrown together by circumstances." He sighed deeply and his lean hands tightened on her shoulders. "I find you damnable attractive, but I've got cold feet."

"You, too?" she mused.

He smiled. "Me, too."

"So, what do we do?"

He let go of her shoulders and took her hand again. "We're two old friends taking a stroll together," he said simply. "We like each other. Period. Nothing heavy. Nothing permanent. Just friends."

"Okay. That suits me."

They walked on down the beach. And if she was disturbed by his closeness, she didn't let it show.

Karie was now talking to an old woman holding four serapes, about a fourth of a mile down the beach from the house.

"Dad!" she cried, running to catch his hand and drag him to the old woman. "I'm glad you're back, did you have a good trip? Listen, you know I can't speak Spanish, and I've got to have this blanket, will you tell her?" she asked in a rush, pointing to an exquisite serape in shades of red and blue.

He chuckled and translated. He spoke the language so beautifully that Janine just drank it in, listening with pleasure.

He pulled out his wallet and paid for the serape, handing it to Karie as the old woman gave them a toothy grin and went back along the beach.

"Don't do that again!" he chided his daughter. "It isn't safe to wander off without letting anyone know where you are."

"Okay, I won't. I spotted her and this blanket was so pretty that I just had to have it. But I couldn't make her understand."

"I'll have to tutor you," he mused.

"Yes, you will, and Kurt, too. I've got to show this to him! Glad you're home, Dad!" she called over her shoulder.

She tore off back down the beach toward Kurt, the serape trailing in the wind.

"You speak Spanish beautifully," Janine said. "How did you learn it so fluently?"

"At my mother's knee," he replied. "I told you that she was from Valladolid, in Spain." He smiled. "I went there when I finally had enough money to travel, and found some cousins I'd never met."

"Were your parents happy together?"

He nodded. "I think so. But my father worked long hours and he wasn't very well. My mother was a cleaning lady for a firm of investment brokers, until she died. I'm sorry Karie had to be torn between two parents. She still loves her mother, as she should. But now there's a stepfather in the picture. And he's a little too 'affectionate' to suit me or Karie. So we find excuses to make sure she has time alone with just her mother."

She lifted her eyes to his. "What happens if he shows up while she's there?"

"Oh, I had a long talk with him," he said easily, and one corner of his mouth curved. "He knows now that I have a nasty temper, and he doesn't want to spend the rest of his life as a soprano. Consequently he'll keep his hands off my daughter. But Marie wants custody, and she's been unpleasant about it in recent months. I've told her how I felt, and she knows what I'll do if she pushes too hard. I may not have money, but I've got a hot temper and plenty of influence in the right places."

She smiled. "Is it really true, that men with Latin blood are hot-tempered and passionate?"

He pursed his thin lips and glanced at her. "If we weren't just old friends, I'd show you."

"But we are, of course. Old friends, that is."

"Of course!"

They walked on down the beach, content in each

other's company. Janine thought absently that she'd never been quite so happy in her life.

They reached the beach house and she started to go up the steps.

"I have to fly to Miami in the morning on business."

"You just got back from New York!" she exclaimed.

"I'm trying to regroup. It's wearing," he explained. "I'm meeting a group of potential investors in Miami. I'm going to take Karie along with me in the Learjet this time. Would you and Kurt like to come?"

Her heart leapt. She could refuse, but her brother would never speak to her again if she turned down a flight in a real baby jet.

"Will the plane hold us all?" she asked with honest curiosity.

"It seats more than four people," he said dryly.

"You'll have to have a pilot and a copilot..."

"I fly myself," he replied. "Don't look so perplexed, I'm instrument rated and I've been flying for many years. I won't crash."

She flushed. "I didn't mean to imply...!"

"Of course you didn't. Want to come?"

She shrugged. "Kurt loves airplanes and flying. If I say no, he'll stake me out on the beach tonight and let the sand crabs eat me."

He chuckled. "Good. I'll come by for you in the morning."

"Thanks."

"*De nada*," he murmured. His eyes narrowed as he studied her. He glanced down the beach, where Karie and Kurt were now oblivious to the world, building a huge sand castle near the discarded serape that Karie seemed to find uninteresting now that she owned it.

"What is it?" she asked when he hesitated.

"Nothing much," he replied, moving closer. "I just wanted to answer that question for you. You know, the one you asked earlier, about men with Latin blood?"

"What quest...!"

His mouth cut the word in half. His arm caught her close against the side of his body, so that she was riveted to him from thigh to breast. His mouth was warm and hard and so insistent that her heart tried to jump right out of her chest. The light kisses that had come before were nothing compared to this one.

Against his mouth, she breathed in the taste of him, felt his teeth nibble sensuously at her upper lip to separate it from the lower one. Then his tongue shot into her mouth, right past her teeth, in an intimacy that corded her body like stretched twine. She stiffened, shivering, frightened by the unexpected rush of pure feeling.

"Easy," he breathed. His slitted eyes looked right into hers. "Don't fight it."

His mouth moved onto hers again, and this time there was nothing preliminary at all about the way he kissed her. She felt the world spinning around her wildly. She held on for dear life, her mouth swelling, burning, aching for his as the kiss went on and on and on.

When his head finally lifted, her nails were biting into the muscles of his shoulders. Her hair was touseled, her eyes misty and wild, all at once, as they met his.

Her mouth trembled from the pressure and passion

of his kiss. He looked down at it with quiet satisfaction.

"Yes," he whispered.

His head bent again, and he kissed her less passionately, tenderly this time, but with a sense of possession.

He let her go, easing her upright again.

She couldn't seem to find words. Her eyes sought reassurance in his, and found only a wall behind which he seemed hidden, remote, uninvolved. Her heart was beating her to death, and he looked unruffled.

"You're young for a woman your age," he remarked quietly.

She couldn't get words out. She was too busy trying to catch her breath.

He touched her swollen lips gently. "I won't do that again," he promised solemnly. "I didn't realize...quite how vulnerable you were." He sighed, brushing back her wild hair. "Forgive me?"

She nodded.

He smiled and dropped his hand. "I'll see you and Kurt in the morning."

"Okay."

He winked and walked back down the beach, totally unconcerned, at least on the surface. Inside he was seething with new emotions, with a turmoil that he didn't dare show to her. Innocence like that couldn't be faked. She wasn't in his league, and he'd better remember it. That sort of woman would expect marriage before intimacy, he knew it as surely as if she'd said it aloud. She wasn't modern or sophisticated. Like her academic parents, she lived in another world from the one he inhabited.

Of course, he was thinking to himself, marriage

wouldn't be so bad if it was with a woman he liked and understood. He laughed at his own folly. Sure. Hadn't he made that very mistake with his first wife? He'd better concentrate on his business empire and leave love to people who could handle it.

All the same, he thought as he entered his house, Janine was heaven to kiss.

Chapter Six

The news that he was going to get to fly in a Learjet made Kurt's head spin. He didn't even sleep that night. The next morning, he was awake at daybreak, waiting for his sister to wake up and get dressed so they could leave.

"He won't be here yet," she grumbled. "It's not even light!"

"All the more reason why we should be ready to go when he does get here," he said excitedly. "A *real* Learjet. My gosh, I still can't believe it!"

"You and airplanes," she mumbled as she made coffee. "Why don't you like bones and things?"

"Why do you like old books?"

"Beats me."

"See?"

She didn't see anything. She was wearing shorts with a white T-shirt, her usual night gear, and neither of her eyes seemed to work. A cup of coffee would fix that, she thought as she made it.

"Do I hear footsteps?" he asked suddenly, jumping up from the table in the kitchenette. "I'll go see if someone's at the door."

Unbelievably it was Canton. "Why don't you go over and keep Karie company while your sister gets ready?" he invited. "She's got cheese danishes and doughnuts."

"Great! Hurry up, sis!" he called over his shoulder.

Janine, still drowsy, turned as Canton came into the small kitchenette area, stifling a yawn. "Sorry. I didn't expect you this early."

"Kurt did," he chuckled.

She smiled. "He barely slept. Want some coffee?"

His eyes slid down to the white T-shirt. Under it, the darkness of her nipples was visible and enticing. As he looked at them, they suddenly reacted with equal visibility.

Janine, shocked, started to cross her arms, but he was too quick for her.

As her arms started to lift, his hands slid under the T-shirt. His head bent. He kissed her as his thumbs slid gently over her soft breasts and up onto the hard tips.

She made a harsh sound. His mouth hardened. He backed her into the wall and held her there with his hips while his hands explored her soft body. All the while, his mouth played havoc with her self-control, with her inhibitions.

"The hell with this," he growled.

While her whirling mind tried to deal with the words, his hands were peeling her right out of the T-shirt. Seconds later, his shirt was unbuttoned and they were together, nude from the waist up, her soft breasts buried in the thick pelt that covered his hard muscles.

She whimpered at the heat of the embrace, at the unexpected surge of passion she'd never experienced before. Her arms locked around his neck and she lifted herself to him, feeling the muscles of his thighs tighten and swell at her soft pressure.

He lifted his mouth a breath away and looked into her eyes from so close that she could see the faint specks of green there in the ocean blue of his eyes.

"What the hell are we doing?" he whispered harshly.

Her eyes fell to his swollen mouth. "At your age, you ought to know," she chided with dry humor.

His hips ground into hers. "Feel that?" he snapped. "If you don't pull back right now, I'll show you a few more things I ought to know at my age."

She was tempted. She never had been so tempted before. Her eyes told him so.

That vulnerability surprised him. He'd expected her to jerk back, to be flustered, to demand an apology. But she wasn't doing any of those things. She was waiting. Thinking. Wondering.

"Curious?" he asked gently.

She nodded, smiling self-consciously.

"So am I," he confessed. He eased away from her, holding her arms at her sides when he moved back so that he could see the exquisite curves of her body. She was firm and her breasts had tilted tips. He smiled, loving their beauty.

"I like looking at you," he said, but after a second, he let her go.

She moved back, picking up her T-shirt. She pulled it on and brushed back her hair, her eyes still curious and disturbed when she looked at him.

He was buttoning his shirt with amused indulgence. "Now you know."

"Know...what?"

"That I'm easy," he murmured, provoking a smile on her lips. "That I can be had for a kiss. I have no self-control, no willpower. You can do whatever you like with me. I'm so ashamed."

She burst out laughing. He was impossible. "I'll just bet you are," she murmured.

He held up a hand. "Don't embarrass me."

"Ha!"

"No kidding. I'm going to start blushing any minute. You just keep that shirt on, if you please, and stop tormenting me with your perfect body."

She searched his eyes, fascinated. She'd never dreamed that intimacy could be fun.

He rested his hands on his hips. "Well, we've established one thing. I know too much and you don't know a damned thing."

"I do now," she replied.

He chuckled. "Not much."

She studied her bare feet. "Care to further my education?"

His heart seemed to stop beating. He hesitated, choosing his words. "Yes."

She lifted her gaze back to his face and searched it quietly. "So?"

"We're flying to Miami," he reminded her.

"I didn't mean right now."

"Good thing. I'm hopeless before I've had two cups of coffee."

She grinned at the obvious humor.

He moved close and took her by the waist. "Listen, we're explosive together. It feels good, but we could get in over our heads pretty quickly. You're not a party girl.''

She frowned. "What do you mean?"

"If you had a modern outlook on life, you wouldn't be a virgin at your age," he said simply. "You're looking for marriage, not a good time. Right?"

"I never thought about it like that."

"You'd better start," he replied. "I want you, but all I have to offer is a holiday affair. I've been married. I didn't like it. I'm free now and I want to stay that way."

"I see."

"This isn't something I haven't said before, Janie," he reminded her. "If you want me, with no strings attached, fine. We'll make love as often as you like. But afterward, I'll go home and never look back. It will be a casual physical fling. Nothing more. Not to me."

She felt confusion all the way to the soles of her feet. She was hungry for him. But was it only physical? Was it misplaced hero worship? And did she want more than a few nights in his arms?

He made her feel uncomfortable. All her adult life she'd spent her days and nights at a computer or with her nose stuck in books. She'd never had the sort of night life that most of her friends had. Intimacy was too solemn a thing for her to consider it casually. But with this man, here, now, she could think of nothing else.

He touched her cheek gently. "Do you want the truth? You're a repressed virgin in the first throes of sexual need, and you're curious. I'm flattered. But after you've spent a night in my arms, no matter how good it is, you're going to have doubts and you're not going to be too happy with yourself for throwing control to the winds. You need to think this through before you do something you might regret. What about the man back in Indiana? Where does he fit in? And if you have an affair with me, how will he feel about you, afterward? Is he the sort of man who'd overlook it?''

"No," she said without thinking.

He nodded. "So don't jump in headfirst."

She sighed. He made it sound so complicated. Imagine, a man who wanted her that much taking time to talk her out of it. Maybe he did care a little, after all. Otherwise, wouldn't he just take what was blatantly offered and go on with his life?

"Just friends," she said with a grin, looking up at him. "Very old friends."

"That's right."

"Okay. But you have to stop kissing me, because it makes me crazy."

"That makes two of us." He stuck his hands into his pockets to keep them off her. "And you have to stop going braless."

"I didn't know you'd be here this early, or I wouldn't be."

He smiled. "Just as well," he confessed. "I wouldn't have missed that for the world."

She chuckled. "Thanks."

"Get dressed, then, would you? Before all this bravado wears off."

She gave him a wicked grin and went to get dressed for the trip.

It was a wonderful, joyful trip. Canton let Kurt sit in the cockpit with him and they talked about airplanes and jets all the way to Miami.

When they got to town, a big white stretch limousine met them at the airport. To Kurt, who was used to traveling in old taxis and beat-up cars, it was an incredible treat. He explored everything, under Canton's amused eyes.

"It's just a long car," he informed the boy. "After a while, they all look alike."

"It's my first time in a limo, and I'm going to enjoy it," he assured him, continuing the search.

Janine, who frequently went on tour and rode around in limos like this, watched her brother with equal amusement. She'd wanted to take him with her on the last trip, but he couldn't lose the time from school. Only illness had gotten him this break.

"Aren't you curious?" Canton asked her. "You seem very much at home in here."

Her eyebrows lifted. "Do I? Actually I'm very excited."

"Are you?"

She smiled sweetly, and turned her attention back to Kurt.

Later, while Canton was in his meeting, Karie and Kurt went to a big mall with Janine, where they peeked and poked through some of the most expensive shops in town. By the time they ended up at an exclusive chocolatier shop and bought truffles, they were all ready to go home.

Canton accepted a chocolate on the way back to the airport, smiling as he tasted it. "My one weakness," he explained. "I love chocolate."

"He's a chocoholic," Karie added. "Once, he went rushing out in the middle of the night for a chocolate bar."

"Sounds just like Janie," Kurt replied with a smile. "She keeps chocolate hidden all over the house."

"Hidden?" Canton probed.

"We stop her from eating it if we find any in her hiding places. She gets terrible migraines when she eats it," he explained. "Not that it ever stopped her. So we have to."

"She's just eaten two enormous truffles," Karie said worriedly.

Janine glared at the kids. "I'm perfectly all right," she informed them. "Anyway, it doesn't *always* give me migraines," she told her brother firmly.

That night, lying in the bed and almost screaming with pain, she remembered vividly what she said to Kurt.

She lost her lunch, and then her supper. The pain was so bad that she wished for a quick and merciful death.

She didn't even realize that Kurt had gone to get Canton until she felt his hand holding hers.

"You don't have anything to take?" he prompted.

"No," she squeaked.

He let go of her hand and called a doctor. Scant minutes later, a dark gentleman in a suit administered a whopping injection. And only a little later, pain gave way to blessed oblivion.

She woke with a weight on her arm. Her eyes opened. Her whole head felt sore, but the headache was so subdued that it was almost a memory.

She looked toward the side of the bed, and there was Canton Rourke, in a burgundy robe, with his face lying on her arm. He was sound asleep, half in a chair and half against her side of the bed.

"Good heavens, what are you doing here?" she croaked.

He heard her, blinking to sudden alertness. He sat up. He needed a shave and his hair was tousled. His eyes were bloodshot. He looked tired to death, but he was smiling.

"Feel better?" he asked.

"Much." She put a hand to her head. "It's very sore and it still hurts a little."

"He left a vial of pills and a prescription for some more. I'm sorry," he added. "I had no idea that Karie would take you to the chocolate shop."

"She couldn't have stopped me," she replied with a pained smile. "They have the best, the most exquisite chocolates on earth. It's my favorite place in the world. And it was worth the headache. Where did you find a doctor in the middle of the night?"

"Karie had appendicitis when we were down here a couple of years ago," he replied. "Dr. Valdez is one of the best, and he has a kind heart."

"Yes, he does. And so do you. Thanks," she said sincerely.

He shrugged. "You'd have done it for me."

She thought about that. "Yes, I would have," she said after a minute.

He smiled.

He stretched largely, wincing as his sore muscles protested.

"Come to bed," she offered with a wan smile, patting the space beside her. "It's too late to go home now."

"I was just thinking the same thing."

He went around to the other side of the bed, but he kept his robe on when he slid under the covers.

"Prude," she accused weakly.

He chuckled drowsily. "I can't sleep normally with Karie anywhere around. Usually I wear pajama bottoms, but they're in the wash, hence the robe."

"That's considerate of you."

"Not really," he confessed. "Actually, I *am* a prude. I don't even like undressing in front of other men." His head turned toward hers. "I was in the Marine Corps. You can't imagine how that attitude went down with my D.I."

She chuckled and then grabbed her head. "Modesty shouldn't be a cardinal sin, even in the armed services."

"That's what I told him."

She took a slow breath. Her head was still uncomfortable.

"Go back to sleep," he instructed, drawing her into his arms. "If it starts up again, wake me and I'll get the pills."

"You're a nice man," she murmured into his shoulder.

"Yes, I am," he agreed. "And don't you forget it. Now go to sleep."

She didn't think she could, with him so close. But the heavy, regular beat of his heart was comforting, as was the warmth of his long, muscular body against her. She let her eyelids fall and seconds later, she slept.

There was a lot of noise. She heard rustling and footsteps and the clanking of metal pans. It all went over her head until something fell with an awful clatter, bringing her eyes open.

"Where the hell are the frying pans? Don't you have a frying pan?" he asked belligerently.

She sat up gingerly, holding her head. "I don't think so," she told him.

"How do you scramble eggs?"

She blinked. "I don't. Nobody here eats them."

"I eat them. And you're going to, as soon as I find a—" he expressed several adjectives "—frying pan!"

"Don't you use that sort of language in my house," she said haughtily.

"I've heard all about your own vocabulary from Kurt, Miss Prim and Proper," he chided. "Don't throw stones."

"I almost never use words like that unless my computer spits out a program or loses a file."

"Computers do neither, programmers do."

"I don't want to understand how a computer works, thank you, I only want it to perform."

He chuckled. "Okay. Now what about pots and pans?"

"It won't do you any good to find one, because I don't have any eggs."

He presented her with a bowl of them. "Our housekeeper came back this morning laden with raw breakfast materials. I even have bacon and freshly baked bread."

"I hope you don't expect me to eat it, because I can't," she murmured weakly. "And I'm going to need some of those pills."

He produced them, along with a small container of bottled water. "Here. Swallow."

She took the pills and lay back down, her eyes bloodshot and swollen. "I feel terrible," she whispered.

"Is it coming back?"

"Yes. It's not so bad as it was yesterday, but it still throbs."

"Stop eating chocolate."

She sighed. "I forget how bad the headaches are when I don't actually have one."

"So Kurt says."

"There are pans in the drawer under the stove," she said helpfully.

He opened it and retrieved a tiny frying pan. He held it up with a sigh. "Well, I guess it'll hold one egg, at least. I have to have an egg. I can't live without an egg every morning, and damn the cholesterol."

"Addictions are hell," she murmured.

He glared at her. "You have to have your coffee, I notice. And we won't mention chocolate..."

"*Please* don't," she groaned.

He shook the frying pan at her. "Next time, I'll go along when you shop. You'll have to get through me to get at any chocolate."

She stared at him with blank eyes. "That sounds very possessive."

He returned her quiet scrutiny. His eyes began to warm. "Yes, it does, doesn't it?" The smile faded. "Just remember. I'm not a marrying man. Not anymore."

"Okay. I promise not to ask you to marry me," she agreed, groaning when movement set her headache off again. She rolled over and held her head with both hands.

"The pills should take effect soon," he said sympathetically. "Have you had coffee yet?"

"No," she whispered.

"That might be making it even worse. Here, I'll get you a cup."

"Excuse me?"

He poured black coffee into a cup, added a little cold water to temper the heat and sat down beside her.

"If you drink coffee all the time, you can get a headache from leaving it off. Caffeine is a drug," he reminded her.

"I know. I remember reading about withdrawal, but I was too sick when I first woke up to want even water."

"Just the same, you'd better have some of the hair of the dog."

"Chocolate has caffeine," she remarked as she sipped the strong coffee. He made it just as she did— strong enough to melt spoons.

"So it does. Want a chocolate truffle?"

She glared at him and sipped another swallow of coffee.

"Sorry," he murmured. "Low blow."

"Wasn't it?" She laid back down with a long sigh. "Why are you being so nice to me?"

"I have a soft spot for problem chocoholics," he gibed. He smiled at her as he got up. "Besides, we're old friends."

"So we are," she mused, wincing with pain.

He tossed the empty eggshells into the garbage can. He searched through drawers until he found a fork. "No wire whip," he muttered.

"I don't torture my food."

He glanced at her. "A wire whip isn't torture. It's an absolute necessity for scrambled eggs and any number of exquisite French cream sauces."

"Listen to the gourmet chef," she exclaimed.

"I can cook. I've done my share of it over the years. I wasn't born rich."

She rolled over on her side to stare at him. "How did you grow up?"

He chuckled. "On the lower east side of Manhattan," he told her. "In a lower middle class home. My father worked long hours to support us."

"Your mother?"

"She died when my younger sister was born," he explained. "I was fourteen. Dad had a boy and an infant girl to raise and pr vide for. He did the best he could, but he wore out when I was seventeen, and I had to take over. He died of lung cancer." He glanced at her. "And, no, he didn't smoke. He worked in a factory brimming over with carcinogens. He wasn't literate or educated, so he did the work he could get."

"I'm sorry. That must have been rough on all of you."

"It was." He stirred the eggs absently. "I took care of him myself for as long as I could. We couldn't afford nursing care. Hell, we couldn't afford a doctor, except at the free clinic." He drew in a long breath. "I was holding down two jobs at the time, one full-time at a printing shop and the other part-time at an investment house, as a janitor." He gave her a long look. "Yes, that's where I learned the ropes. One of the older executives lost his son in a traffic accident in New Jersey about the same time my father died. He worked late and we ran into each other occasionally and talked. Eventually, when he found out how hard it was for me, he started teaching me about money. By God, he made an investment wizard out of me, long before I started designing software and linked up with the ex-NASA guys. And I never even got to thank him. He dropped dead of a heart attack before I made my first million.'' He shook his head. ''Ironic, how things work out.''

''Yes.'' She watched him move. He had an elegance of carriage, a sensuous arrogance that made him a pleasure to watch. Muscles rippled in his arms and chest under the close fitting knit shirt and slacks he wore. ''Are you still close to your sister?''

He didn't answer for a minute. ''My sister died of a drug overdose when she was sixteen. It was my fault.''

Chapter Seven

"What do you mean, it was your fault?" she asked, curious.

"She got in with a bad crowd. I didn't even know," he said. "I was just too damned busy—working, trying to stay afloat with Marie, being a new dad, all those things. I tried to keep an eye on her. But I didn't know who she was dating. It turned out that she was in a relationship with our neighborhood drug dealer. He was her supplier. One night, she took too much. They called me from the emergency room. The rat took off the minute she went into cardiac arrest."

"He got clean away, I gather?"

Canton stirred eggs until they cooked, and then took them off the stove before he answered. "No, he didn't," he said deliberately, "although it took me a few years to get rich enough to go looking for him. He's doing ten years on a dealing charge. I hired private detectives to watch him. It didn't take long to catch him with enough evidence to send him up. But it didn't bring her back.''

She could sense his pain. She sat up in bed, grimacing as the movement hurt her head. ''I know. But there's only so much you can do to keep people out of trouble. If they really want to hurt themselves, you can't stop them, no matter how much you love them.''

He glanced at her over the eggs he'd just spooned onto a plate. ''You see deeper than most people. Much deeper.''

She shrugged. ''That can make life pretty hard sometimes.''

''It can make it worth living, as well.''

She smiled back. ''I suppose so.''

''I don't suppose you have a toaster?''

''Waste of money,'' she said. ''The toast never comes out warm enough to butter. I make it in the oven broiler.''

''That's what I was afraid of.''

All the same, he accomplished cinnamon toast with a minimum of fuss, though, and then spoon-fed her delicious scrambled egg and a bite of toast with some strong black coffee.

She smiled as he put the empty plate aside. ''You're a nice man,'' she said.

''You needn't sound so surprised,'' he replied. ''I'm just a man.''

''A man who built an empire all alone,'' she elaborated.

''I had plenty of help. The problem is that when people get famous, they stop being people to the public. I'm no different than when I used to get my little sister up and ready for school. I'm just older and better dressed.''

"People get lost in the glamour, I guess," she agreed.

"All too often, they do. Making money is mostly just plain hard work and sacrifice. No sane person would do anything to excess just to make money."

"Then why did you?" she asked.

"For fun," he replied. "I love creating computer software. It's a challenge to combine numbers and logic and make a new program from scratch that does exactly what you want it to. I never thought about making money."

She chuckled softly. "But you did."

"A hell of a lot of it," he said, nodding. "And it was nice, while it lasted. But you know what?" he added, leaning closer. "I'm just as happy now, with the challenge of making it all back again."

She understood that. It was the same with her, when she wrote a book. She wondered what he'd say if he knew what she did for a living, that she'd deceived him into thinking she was just a secretary on holiday. His opinion of famous women wasn't very high. Of course, she wasn't all that famous. And he wasn't in love with her, either. Perhaps she was making a problem of it.

"You look pale," he remarked. He smoothed back her hair, concern in his blue eyes as he studied her wan, drawn face. "You've had a hard night. Why don't you try and get some sleep? I'll watch Kurt for you."

"Thanks. I think it might help."

He drew the sheet over her. "I'll lock up on my way out. Has Kurt got a key?"

"Yes. But he won't remember where he put it. It's

in his windbreaker pocket that zips up. It's on the couch.''

"I'll take it with me." He bent and kissed her forehead gently. "Will you be all right alone, or do you want me to stay?"

"I'll be fine now," she promised. She smiled drowsily, because the pills were starting to take effect. "Thanks."

He shrugged. "Old friends help each other out," he reminded her.

"I'll remember that if you're ever in trouble."

He looked funny for a minute. She reached up and touched his dark hair. "Doesn't anyone look after you?"

"Karie tries to, I guess."

"No one else?"

He thought about that. "Actually no," he said finally.

She traced his high cheekbone. "Then I will, when I'm better."

He gave her an inscrutable look and got to his feet, frowning. "I'll check on you later. Need anything else?"

"No. And thanks for breakfast. You're not a bad cook."

"Anyone can scramble eggs."

"Not me."

"I'll teach you one of these days. Sleep tight."

She lay back and closed her eyes. He cleaned up the kitchen quickly and efficiently, and then went out and locked the door behind him.

By early afternoon, Janine was improved enough to get up and dress, which she did, in jeans and a white tank top.

"God, you're young," he remarked when she joined him in the living room.

Her eyebrows lifted. She was still pale, and wore only a little pink lipstick. "I beg your pardon?"

"You're young," he muttered, hands deep in the pockets of his loose-fitting slacks. His blue eyes had narrowed as he studied her lithe figure and her blemishless complexion.

"Twenty-four isn't exactly nursery-school age," she said pointedly. "And you aren't over the hill."

He chuckled. "I feel it, sometimes. But, thanks, anyway."

She averted her eyes. "You must know that you're devastating physically."

There was a silence that eventually made her look at him. His face had tautened, his eyes had gone glittery. Their intent stare made her pulse leap.

His chin lifted almost imperceptibly. "Come here," he said in a deep, velvety tone.

Her legs obeyed him at once, even though her mind was protesting what amounted to nothing less than an order.

But when he reached for her, it didn't matter. Nothing mattered, except the pressure of his arms around her and the insistent, devouring hunger of the hard mouth on hers.

She leaned into him with a sigh, all hope of self-protection gone. It could have led anywhere, except that young, excited voices floated in through the patio door, warning of the imminent arrival of the kids.

He let her go with obvious reluctance. "I could get addicted to your mouth," he said huskily.

"I was thinking the same thing," she agreed with a breathless laugh.

"Don't get your hopes up," he mused, glancing toward the door where footsteps grew louder. "We'd have better luck on the floor of Grand Central Station."

"I noticed."

Before she could add anything else, Kurt and Karie came running into the beach house carrying some huge feathers.

"Where did you get those?" Janine asked.

"A guy was selling them on the beach. Do you know where we can get a skeleton?"

She blinked. "A what?"

"Not a real one." Kurt cleared his throat. "Karie and I are sort of studying anatomy. We need a skull. Or something."

"They sell cow skulls at the *mercado* in town." Canton reached into his pocket and produced two twenty-dollar bills. "That ought to do it."

"Okay. Thanks, Dad!" Karie exclaimed. "How about cab fare to town?"

He produced more bills. "Come right back," he said firmly. "And if you get lost, find a policeman and have him call me."

"Will do. Thanks!"

They were off at a dead run again. Janine and Canton stood on the deck and watched them head toward the front of the house. A movement caught Janine's attention.

There he was again.

The dark man was standing near the front of the house, beside a sedan. The kids hailed a taxi that had just come from one of the big hotels on a nearby spit of land. They climbed in and as Janine watched in barely contained horror, the dark man climbed into his vehicle and proceeded to follow the cab.

"Did you see that?" she asked her companion worriedly.

"See what?" he asked.

"A man got into a car and followed the cab."

He frowned. "I didn't notice the man. What was he driving?"

"Some old beat-up sedan. I've seen it before." She grimaced. "It probably wasn't a good idea to let them go off alone. If my parents have found something major, who knows what a determined pothunter might do? What if someone's after Kurt?" she suggested.

He took in a deep breath and rammed his hands deep into his pockets. "I was just thinking the same thing, but too late. I'll go after them. Don't worry. Even a pothunter would think twice about abducting an American child right off the streets of Cancún."

"I'm not so sure."

She paced the floor until Canton returned with the children in tow. They had their skull and were content to stay on the beach and study it. Janine was worried, though, and not only about the mysterious dark man. She was worried because Canton seemed to deliberately downplay the incident, as if it didn't really concern him very much. She wondered why, because he looked much more preoccupied than she'd seen him before.

"I was too sick to ask before. How did it go in Miami with your investors?" she asked after she'd fixed them a pot of coffee.

"I did better than I expected to," he replied. "Apparently they think I can pull it off."

"I agree with them."

He searched her eyes and smiled. "Nice of you."

She shrugged. "You're that sort of man. I'll bet your employees are crazy about you."

"I offered you a job, I seem to recall," he mused. "Come work for me. I'll make you rich."

"I'm not sure I want to be." She glanced up. "Money isn't everything, but it must be a help when you have death-defying parents." She drew in a long breath. "And I still haven't heard from them. I phoned the university this morning. They haven't heard anything, either."

"How do they contact you?"

"There's a small satellite link they use in the field," she explained. "They can send me E-mail anytime they like. But even the local guide service hasn't been able to contact them. I haven't told Kurt. I thought it best not to. This is a big deal, this new site. I couldn't bear it if anything's happened to them."

"Why didn't you say something before?" he muttered. "I may not have millions, but I have influence. Give me that phone."

It was impossible to follow what he was saying, but one of the names he mentioned in his conversation was very recognizable.

"You know the president of Mexico?" she exclaimed when he hung up.

"You don't speak Spanish," he reminded her, "so how did you know that?"

"I recognized his name," she returned. "Do you know him?"

"Yes, I know him. They're going to send someone right out in an aircraft to look for your parents. I'd go myself, but the Learjet isn't ideal for this sort of search."

"How will they know where to look?"

"They had to contact the appropriate government agency to get permission to excavate, didn't they?"

She smiled her relief. "Of course they did. Thank you," she added belatedly.

"Don't mention it. Now drink your coffee."

By the end of the day, there was a telephone call. It was brief and to the point, but welcome.

"They're fine," Canton told a nervous Janine when he put down the receiver. "Their communications equipment had a glitch, and they had to send a runner to the nearest town to fetch an electronics man. He only arrived today. No problems."

"Oh, thank God," she said fervently.

He smiled at her rakishly. "Don't I get anything?"

She moved toward him. "What would you like?" she asked, aware that the kids were close by, sitting on the darkened deck, watching some people down the beach play music and dance in the sand. "A reward?"

"That would be nice," he murmured when she reached him.

"A gift certificate?" she suggested.

His hands framed her face and lifted it. "I had something a little more...physical...in mind."

She felt as breathless as she sounded when she spoke. "How physical?" she whispered.

"Nothing dire." His mouth covered hers and he kissed her softly, sweetly, deeply. His arms enveloped her gently and the kiss grew to a shattering intensity in the soft silence of the room.

He let her go by breaths. "You're a drug," he breathed shakily.

"I know. So are you." She moved closer, only to find herself firmly put away.

"You're the marrying kind," he reminded her. "I'm not."

"It might not matter."

"It would," he said.

She sighed heavily. "Prude."

He chuckled. "Count on it. Your lipstick is smudged."

"I don't doubt it." She ran a finger around her mouth and fixed the smear. "I'll bet you make love like a pagan."

He smiled slowly, confidently. He leaned toward her slightly, and his voice lowered to a deep purr. "I do."

Her eyes lowered demurely. "Show me," she whispered.

He was barely breathing at all, now. His fists clenched by his side. "This isn't a game. Don't tease."

She looked up again, saw his eyes glitter, his jaw clenched as tightly as the lean hands in fists on his thighs.

"I'm not teasing," she said quietly. "I mean it. Every word."

"So do I," he replied. "I am not, repeat *not*, taking you to bed."

She threw up her hands. "Are you always so cautious? Is that how you made those millions?"

"I don't mind a calculated risk, with money. I mind one with human bodies. Mistakes happen in the heat of passion. I'm not taking chances with you, ever.

You're going to marry some normal, steady man like your professor boyfriend and live happily ever after.''

"Is that an order?"

"You bet!"

She searched his face with sad eyes. "I'd only spend the rest of my life dreaming about you."

"It's the glamour," he said flatly. "If I were a poor man, or a wage earner, you'd feel differently. Hell, I can look in a mirror! I know what women see, without the glitter. You're a working girl and I've been a multimillionaire. A little hero worship is inevitable."

"You think I'm attracted to your wallet?" she exclaimed on a hushed laugh. Only a working girl! She was world famous. He didn't know that, though.

"No, I don't think you're a gold digger," he said emphatically. "But I do think that you're attracted to an image that doesn't really exist."

"Images don't kiss like you do."

"I'm leaving. I don't like losing arguments."

"Neither do I. Stay and finish this one."

He shook his head. "Not a chance. Get some sleep. I'll see you tomorrow. Karie!" He raised his voice. "Time to go!"

"Coming, Dad!"

He walked out the front door, joined immediately by Karie. They called good-nights over their shoulders, leaving Janine and Kurt by themselves. The room seemed to close in around them.

"Mom and Dad are fine," she told her young brother, putting an affectionate arm around his shoulders as they watched the Rourkes stroll down the beach toward their own house. "Canton called the president's office and they sent out a search party."

He whistled. "Nice to have influence, huh?"

"Nice for us," she agreed. "It's a relief to know they haven't been kidnapped or something."

"You bet!" He glanced up at her. "He reads your books, did you know?"

Her heart jumped. *Canton Rourke?*

"Karie says he's got everything you've ever written, including *Catacomb*. Good thing he hasn't looked at the photo."

"He wouldn't recognize me if he did," she said. "I hope."

"Why don't you tell him?" he asked curiously.

She grimaced. "It's too late for me to tell him now. He'd want to know why I didn't before." She shifted. "He doesn't like famous women."

"He likes you. It won't matter."

"Think not? I wonder," she said thoughtfully.

"He's a great guy."

"So Karie says." She remembered the car following them, then, at the mention of his friend. She glanced down at him. "Have you seen that dark man again, the one I attacked on the beach?"

"Why, yes, I have. He was in town when we were at the *mercado*," Kurt said. "He saw us watching him and took off when I walked toward a policeman."

"I don't like it."

"Neither do I. He's after something. Reckon it's us or Mom and Dad?" he queried.

"I don't know. I'm going to pay more attention to what's going on around us, though, you can count on that."

She went to bed, but the memory of Canton's kisses kept her awake far too long. She got up, dressed in her long white embroidered gown and strolled out onto the deck.

In the moonlight, she saw a figure on the beach, turned toward the Rourke house. Something glinted in the moonlight, something like metal. Could it be a telescope? There was a light on in Canton's living room. There was a figure silhouetted against the curtains. The glint flashed again. Her heart jumped. What if it was a gun, trained on Canton?

She never thought of consequences. Without a thought for her own safety, she darted up to the front of the Rourke home and then rushed out from the side of it toward the man, yelling as she went.

The man was surprised, as she expected, but he reacted much too quickly. He raised an arm and motioned. Before Janine could slow her steps, before she even realized what was coming, two men shot out of the darkness with a sheet. It went over her head and around her. There was a sharp blow to her head, and after the pain came oblivion.

She woke up with a splitting headache and nausea. The floor rocked under her, and her bed was unusually hard. She opened her eyes and rolled over, right onto the hard floor. As she righted herself, she saw where she was. This wasn't her house. It was a boat, a big cabin cruiser, and the dark man who'd been stalking the children was suddenly there, yelling furiously at his two shorter, darker companions. They seemed to be pleading with him, their hands raised in supplication. He wasn't responding. He shouted at them even more.

She groaned involuntarily and they looked toward her menacingly. She knew then, at once, that if she didn't keep her head, she was going to die, right here.

The tall, dark man had a pistol tucked into his belt, and his hand suddenly rested on it.

She closed her eyes and pretended to be unconscious. If he knew that she saw and recognized him, she had little doubt that she'd be a goner. A minute later, she was tossed onto the bunk and rolled over. Her hands were tied firmly behind her.

"No es la muchacha Rourke, ¡idiotas! Es una mujer—es el otra, la vecina," the tall man raged at them.

She didn't understand Spanish, but the words "Rourke girl" and "not" were fairly familiar after two weeks in Mexico. They thought she was Karie! They'd meant to kidnap Karie, and because she'd run out from the Rourke house, in the darkness they'd mistaken her for Karie. They'd got the wrong person. God in heaven, they were after Karie!

The child's life might depend on her now. If they were willing to go to these lengths, to kidnapping at gunpoint, to get Karie, they were deadly serious about what they meant to do. A potential witness, Janine might become expendable any minute. She had to get away, she had to warn Canton and Karie. The reason behind the kidnapping wasn't important right now, but warning them was.

She pretended to sleep. The men stood over her, talking quickly. The tall one muttered something that sounded ominous and his companions agreed with whatever he'd said and followed him up on deck.

The noise of a motor sounded, but not loudly enough to be that of the cabin cruiser itself. This was a big, expensive ship. Obviously there was a small launch used for getting to and from shore. There was money behind this attempted kidnapping. The question was, whose, and what did they stand to profit by it? Canton had no money, at least, not yet. Perhaps he had a trust or a Swiss bank account about which no one knew anything.

Her heart raced madly as she relaxed her arms and wrists. She'd deliberately tensed them while she was being bound, an old trick her karate teacher had taught her. Now the bonds were much looser than they would have been. It would take time and concentration to get them off, but she had a chance. God willing, she'd get free. Then she could worry about how to escape. If the boat was close to shore, she could probably swim it. If there was no riptide, that was. A riptide might carry her miles off course. And if it were possible to swim to shore, why was a launch needed by her captors?

She couldn't waste time worrying about that, she decided. First things first. She'd get loose. Then she'd figure out how to get off the ship.

All she needed now was luck and a little time.

Chapter Eight

The ropes were tied securely. After several minutes of twisting and turning and contorting, she couldn't manage to loosen them even enough to get a finger free, much less an entire hand.

It was like one of her books, she thought with dark humor, but by this point, her heroine would be free and giving her captors hell.

Janine hated reality.

There was the sound of the launch returning, and suddenly she knew real fear. The man had a gun. He was impatient, and angry that the kidnapping had gone awry. He might shoot her. It might be the only way for him.

She thought about her parents and Kurt. She thought about Canton. Death had never been a preoccupation of hers, but now she couldn't escape it. She might die here, in her nightgown, without ever having the chance to say goodbye to the people she loved most. And almost that bad was the realization that the sequel to

Catacomb was barely one third of the way finished. They'd give it to another writer to finish. Oh, the horror of it!

As she gave renewed effort to her attempt to get away, she heard voices again, and suddenly the door of the cabin opened. The tall man was back, wearing a ski mask and gloves. Obviously he didn't think she'd been conscious enough to recognize him before, so he was disguised. That was hopeful. If he meant to kill her, he wouldn't need a disguise. But there was a pistol in his hand. He moved toward her, noting that she was wide-awake and watching him.

With a rasp in his voice, he ordered her, in thickly accented English, to stand up. He marched her ahead of him to the starboard side of the big cabin cruiser, and prodded her toward the rail.

"Jump," he commanded.

There was no launch below. It looked a frightfully long way to the water, and her hands were still tied.

"I'm not going to jump like this, with my hands tied!" she raged at him.

The gun was prodded firmly into her back. She felt a pressure on her bound wrists, and they were suddenly free, a knife having parted them.

"Get off the boat or die," the voice said harshly. "This is the only chance you'll get."

She didn't wait around to argue. She was a strong swimmer and there was a moon. It wasn't that far to shore. She could see the lights of the beach houses from here. Odd, lights at this hour of the morning…

The pistol punched her spine. She said a quick prayer, stood on the rail with her arms positioned and dived into the water.

It was cooler than she expected, but not so bad once

she accustomed herself to the water. She struck out for shore, her heart throbbing as she waited to see if the man would shoot her in the back once she was on her way. If he was willing to kidnap a child, what would stop him from murdering a potential witness? He was wearing a ski mask now, though; he must have thought that she hadn't had a good look at him. She'd never opened her eyes fully just after she'd regained consciousness. That might save her life.

She swam, counting each stroke, not even pausing for breath as she went steadily toward shore.

There was one bad place where she felt the surge of the waves, but she managed to get through it by relaxing her body and letting the waves sweep her on toward the beach.

She was getting tired. The blow to her head, the disorientation, the lack of sleep all combined dangerously to make her vulnerable to the effort she was expending. She rolled onto her back, floating, while above her the moon made a halo through the clouds. It looked unreal, all gossamer. She was trying to recall some lines about moons and silver apples when she heard a splashing sound close by. All at once, an arm snaked around her head, under her jaw, and she cried out.

"I've got you," Canton's deep voice rasped at her ear. "I'm going to tow you to shore. Are you all right?"

"Head hurts," she whispered. "They hit me."

"Good God!" He turned and struck out for the shore. He was a much more powerful swimmer than she was, each stroke more forceful than the last as he made his way through the waves to the shallows where he could finally stand up.

He tugged her along with him, fighting the powerful undertow. When he was through it, he bent and lifted her sopping wet form in the gown and started toward her beach house.

"The lights...are on," she managed to say weakly.

"I heard you yell," he said curtly. "You weren't in your bed or anywhere else. I've been searching for almost an hour. It only just occurred to me that the cabin cruiser was sitting out there anchored. It's gone now, but I've got the police after it. I thought you were on it. I was watching it with binoculars when I saw you come on deck with someone and jump off."

"I didn't jump. He pushed me off," she said. Every step he took jarred her poor head. She touched her temple. "Oh, dear God, I'm so tired of headaches! That animal hit me over the head!"

His arms contracted. He didn't speak, but his silence was eloquent.

"It's a miracle you didn't drown," he said through his teeth. "By God, someone's going to pay for this!"

"They're after Karie," she whispered, clutching at his soaked shirt. "I heard the tall man mention her name. It's the same man, the one who was...following the kids."

His face went even harder. "Marie," he muttered. "I couldn't meet her financial demands, so she's stooped to kidnapping to make me fork up the money she wants. Damn her!"

"She wouldn't hurt Karie," she mumbled.

"Not intentionally. But they hit you thinking you were Karie, didn't they?"

"I'm afraid so."

He muttered something else and carried her up into her darkened beach house.

"Kurt isn't awake?" she asked worriedly.

"No." He went through to her bedroom, stood her by the bed, stripped her quite forcefully and deftly and stuck her under the covers without a word. "Stay right there until I change clothes. I'm taking you in to the hospital."

"But Karie..." she moaned.

"We'll all go. I'll wake Kurt on my way out. No nausea?" he asked, hesitating in the doorway. For the first time, she saw that he had on trousers and a shirt, but no shoes. "No confusion?"

"Not yet..."

"I'll be right back."

She heard him bang on Kurt's door, heard her brother's thready reply. Her head throbbed so that she couldn't think at all. Kurt came into the room, worried and nervous when he saw her white face.

"What happened?" he exclaimed.

"Some men kidnapped me and took me out to a cabin cruiser," she rasped. "Kurt, put that wet gown in the bathtub and get me a nightgown out of my drawer, please."

"Kidnapped you?"

"They thought...I was Karie, you see," she muttered. She held her head. "Boy, am I going to have a headache now."

"How did they get you?" he persisted.

"I went out when I saw moonlight glinting on a gun barrel. I thought they were going to shoot Canton."

"And you rushed in to the rescue." He shook his head. "I wish I could convince you that you aren't Diane Woody," he groaned, "before you die trying to act like her."

"I got the point, just now," she assured him. "The gown?"

"Sure."

He carried the gown off to the bathtub and didn't come back. Canton did, dressed and impatient. "Where are your clothes?" he demanded, and started looking for them before she could answer him. "These will do."

He closed the door, tossed her underwear to her and jerked the covers off. "No time for a bath right now," he said. "You'll have to go as you are. Here." He helped her into her underthings as if he'd done it all his life. He slid a cool cotton sundress over her head, slid sandals onto her bare feet, then picked her up and strode out of the room with her. It was all too quick for her to feel embarrassment, but she was certain that she would, later.

"I want my purse and my makeup," she said weakly.

"You don't need either. I'm not flat broke and you're too sick for makeup."

"I look awful without it," she whispered weakly.

"That's a matter of perspective." He called to Kurt. The boy had just finished wringing out her gown. He came running, and locked the door behind them before they all went to Canton's waiting rental car. Karie was already in the front seat, wide-awake and concerned when she saw Janine.

"Is she going to be all right?" she asked quickly.

"Of course she is." Canton helped her into the back seat and motioned Kurt in beside her.

He drove like a madman to the hospital, ignoring traffic signs and other motorists. His set expression kept the children from asking any more questions.

He strode right into the emergency room with Janine in his arms and started shooting orders in Spanish right and left the minute he got through the doorway.

In no time at all, Janine was tested for everything from blood loss to concussion and placed in a private room.

"Slight concussion without complications," Canton said a minute later, dropping into a chair beside her bed.

"The kids?" she murmured drowsily.

"Down the hall. They have a guest room."

"What about you?" she persisted.

He took her cool hand in his and leaned back, still holding it. "I'm not leaving you for a second," he murmured, closing his eyes.

She felt warm all over, protected and cherished. Her fingers curled trustingly into his and clung. They must have given her something in that shot, she thought as the world began to recede. She was certainly sleepy.

It was daylight when she woke. Canton was standing by the window, his back to it, staring at her in the bed. Her eyes opened and she looked across at him with slowly returning consciousness.

She felt as if she'd known him all her life. The odd feeling brought a smile to her face.

He didn't return it. His eyes were wary now, watchful. "How are you feeling?" he asked, and even the tone of his voice was different.

"Better. I think," she qualified.

His hands were in his pockets. He didn't move any closer to the bed. His face was drawn, his jaw taut.

While she pondered his sudden change of attitude, the door opened and a nurse came in.

"I'm just going off duty," she said. She had a book

under her arm and she approached the bed a little shyly. "I won't bother you right now, I know you're still feeling under the weather. But I bought *Catacomb* as soon as it came out and it's just the most wonderful mystery I've ever read. I recognized you the minute I saw you, even though the photo in the back is pretty vague. I know your real name, you see, as well as your pen name. I have all your books." She moved closer, smiling shyly at Canton. "I was telling Mr. Rourke what a thrill it was to get to see you in person. I don't want to intrude or anything. I just wondered if I left my book, if you'd sign it? I put a slip of paper with my name inside the cover. If you don't mind."

"I don't mind," Janine said with a wan smile. "I'll be glad to."

"Thank you!" The young nurse laid the book on the bedside table, flushing. "It's a pleasure. I mean it. I just think you're wonderful! I hope you get better very soon. Thank you again. I really appreciate it. Gosh, you look just like I pictured you!"

She rushed out the door, going off duty, with stars in her eyes. Janine looked toward the door with painful realization.

"So you know," she said without looking at him.

"You could have told me. You knew I read your books. I had *Catacomb* on the side table at my party."

"I knew. Karie told Kurt that you read my books." She studied her hands. "You'd said that you hated famous women, authoresses and actresses." She shrugged, still not meeting his eyes. "I didn't know how to tell you after that."

He didn't speak. His eyes were stormy.

"Did the nurse tell you?"

"No," he said, surprising her into looking up.

"Kurt spilled the beans. He was upset. He said that you got into the worst scrapes because you thought you were your own heroine. I asked what he meant, and Karie said you were acting like Diane Woody." He took a slow breath. "It wasn't much of a jump after that. The nurse had brought your book with her to read on her breaks. She saw you and recognized you at once when they brought you onto her ward."

"A conspiracy."

He laughed without humor. "Of a sort. Fate."

She didn't know what to say. The man who'd taken such exquisite, tender care of her now seemed to want nothing more to do with her. She was sorry that he'd had to find it out the hard way. But they had more immediate problems than her discovered identity.

"What about the men who kidnapped me?" she asked, changing the subject.

"They're being hunted" was all he had to say.

"They weren't after my parents at all," she remarked after a long silence. "But I'm sorry they're trying to take Karie."

"I've put on some extra security."

"Good idea."

He was still glaring in her direction. "Kurt told me what you did."

"I have a bad habit of rushing in headfirst," she said.

"You thought the man had a gun aimed at me," he continued relentlessly.

She cleared her throat. "It looked like it. It was probably a pair of binoculars, but I couldn't be sure."

"So instead of yelling for help, you rushed him. Brilliant!"

She blushed. "You could be dead instead of yelling at me!"

"So could you!" he raged, losing his temper. "Are you a complete loon?"

"Don't you call me names!"

He went toward her and she picked up the nearest thing to hand, a plastic jug full of ice, ready to heave.

He stopped and her hand steadied.

Into the standoff came Kurt and Karie, stopping in the doorway at once when they realized what was going on.

"He's the good guy," Kurt said pointedly.

"That's what you think!" she retorted, wide-eyed and furious.

"Put the jug down," Kurt entreated, moving to her side. "You're in no condition to fight."

He took the jug away from her.

"The voice of reason," she muttered as she gave it to him.

"The still, small voice of reason," he agreed with a grin. "Feeling better?"

"I was," she said darkly, glaring toward Canton.

His expression wasn't readable at all. "I have some things to do," he said. "I'll leave Kurt here with you for the time being."

"When can I go home?" she asked stiffly.

"Later today, if there are no complications."

"I have to have someone translate for me, about insurance and so forth."

"The nurses speak English," he stated. "So do the people in the front office."

"Fine."

He gave her one last, long look and motioned to his

daughter. He didn't say goodbye, get well, so long, or anything conventional. He just left with Karie.

"It's my fault," Kurt said miserably. "I spilled the beans."

"It was inevitable that someone would," she reassured him. "No harm done. A millionaire and a writer are a poor combination at best."

"He isn't a millionaire."

"He will be, again. I don't move in those circles. I never did."

"He stayed in here all night," he said.

She shrugged. "He felt responsible for me, I suppose. That was kind of him." She squared her shoulders. "But I can take care of myself now." She glanced at him. "You didn't try to contact Mom and Dad about this?" she asked with concern.

He shook his head. "We thought we'd wait."

"Thank God!" She sat up. Her head still throbbed. She lay back down against the pillow with a rough sigh. "I wonder what he hit me with," she said. "It must have been something heavy."

"The doctor said it was a light concussion and you were lucky. From now on, let the police do hero stuff, okay?"

She chuckled. "I suppose I'd better."

She stayed one more night in the hospital, this time with Kurt for company. The next morning, she did all the necessary paperwork and checked herself out early.

They went back to the beach house in a cab, arriving just as Canton Rourke and his daughter were getting into their rental car.

She paid the cabdriver, being careful not to look at

Canton. It did no good. He came storming across the sandy expanse with fierce anger in his lean face.

"Just what the hell are you doing home?" he demanded. "I was on my way to the hospital to get you."

"How was I to know that?" she asked belligerently. She was still pale and wobbly, despite her determination to come home. "You left with no apparent intention of returning. I can take care of myself."

He looked vaguely guilty. His eyes went to Karie. He motioned her back into the house. She waved and obeyed.

"I'll go talk to Karie while you two argue," Kurt said helpfully, grinning irrepressibly as he ambled toward Karie's house.

"Everybody's deserting me," she muttered, turning toward the house, purse in hand. Kurt had asked Canton to bring it to the hospital the morning after Janine had regained consciousness, and he had. The money had been a godsend, because she had to get a cab to the house.

"I wouldn't have, if you'd leveled with me from the beginning. I hate being lied to."

She turned on him. "You have no right to ask questions about me. You're not a member of my family or even a close friend. What makes you think I owe you the story of my life?"

He looked taken aback. His shoulders moved under the thin fabric of his gray jacket. "I don't know. But you do. I want to know everything about you," he said surprisingly.

"Why bother to find out?" she asked. "I'll be gone in less than a month, and we're not likely to run into each other again. I don't move in your circles. I may be slightly famous, but I'm not a millionaire, nor likely to be. I keep to myself. I'm not a social animal."

"I know." He smiled gently. "You don't like crowds, or life in the fast lane. Marie did. She felt dead without noise and parties. She liked to go out, I liked to stay home." He shrugged. "We were exact opposites." His blue eyes narrowed. "On the other hand, you and I have almost too much in common."

"I've already told you, I'm not going to propose to you," she said solemnly. "I like being independent. You need to find a nice, quiet, loving woman to cook you scrambled eggs while you're fighting your way back up the corporate ladder. Someone who likes being yelled at," she added helpfully.

"I didn't yell."

"Yes, you did," she countered.

"If I did, you deserved it," he returned shortly. "Running after armed felons, for God's sake! What were you thinking?"

"That I was going to make a citizen's arrest, for one thing." She searched his lean face. "You say you've read my books. Didn't you read the book jackets?"

"Of course," he muttered.

"Then tell me what I did for a living before I started writing novels."

He had to think for a minute. He frowned. His eyes widened and dilated. "For God's sake! I thought that was hype."

"It was not," she replied. "I was a card-carrying private detective. I'm still licensed to carry a weapon, although I don't, and I haven't forgotten one single thing I know about law enforcement."

"That's how you learned the martial arts."

She nodded. "And how to approach a felon, and how to track a suspect. I was doing just fine until the would-be kidnapper pointed a gun at you and I did something stupid. I rushed right in without thinking."

"And it almost got you killed," he added.

"A miss is as good as a mile. Thank God I have a hard head."

He nodded. He touched her hair gently. "I'm sorry I yelled."

She shrugged.

"I mean it," he stated with a smile.

She sighed. "Okay."

She was a world away from him now. He wasn't sure that he could breach the distance, but he had thought of a way to try. "Are you still a licensed private investigator?"

She nodded.

"Then why don't you come to work for me and help me crack this case?"

She pursed her lips. "I'm on a deadline," she said pointedly.

"You can't work all the time."

She considered it. It was exciting to chase a perpetrator. But more important than the thrill of the chase was to prevent someone from taking Karie away. Just thinking about that blow on the head made her furious. They'd thought she was Karie and they had no qualms about hurting her physically. They needed to be stopped, before they did something to harm the child.

"I'll do it," she said.

He grinned. "I can't pay you just yet. But I'll give you a pocketful of I.O.U.s. I promise they'll be redeemable one day."

She chuckled. "I believe it. Okay. That's a deal, then. But I'll need a couple of days to rest up." She touched the back of her head. "I've still got a huge bump."

"No wonder," he muttered, glowering at her. "You are a nut."

"Hiring me doesn't entitle you to call me names," she declared.

He held up both hands. "Okay, I'll reform."

He didn't. He kept muttering all the while several days later while they were lying in wait for the perpetrators to try again, her deadlines forgotten in the excitement of the chase.

"This is so damned boring," he grumbled after they'd been lying behind a sand dune, watching the kids build sand castles for over two hours.

"Welcome to the real live world of detective work," she replied. "You watch too much television."

His head turned and his lips pursed as he studied her. "So do you. Particularly of the science fiction variety."

She glared at him. "That's hitting below the belt."

"Is that any way to talk to a man of my rank and station?" he asked. His lips pursed. "I could have you interrogated, you know," he said in the same mocking tone her favorite series TV character used. He cocked one eyebrow to enhance the effect. "I could do it myself. I have a yen for brunettes."

She cleared her throat. "Stop that."

"Hitting you in your weak spot, hmmm?" he taunted.

"I don't have any weak spots," she replied.

He moved closer, rolling her over onto her back. "That's what you think." He bit off the words against her shocked mouth.

Chapter Nine

For just an instant she gave in to her longing for him and lay back, floating on waves of pure bliss as his mouth demanded everything she had to give. His lean body fit itself to hers and delicious thrills ran down her spine. She moaned, pulling him closer, the danger forgotten as she gave in to her hunger for him.

But her sense of self-preservation was too well developed not to assert itself eventually. When his thigh began to ease her long legs apart, she stiffened and wriggled away quickly, with a nervous laugh.

"Cut that out," she murmured. "We're on a case here."

He was breathing roughly, his eyes glittery with amusement and something deeper. "Spoilsport," he said huskily. "Besides, you were the one trying to seduce me a few days ago."

She put her hand over her wildly beating heart. "Scout's honor, I won't try it again," she promised.

His eyes narrowed. "I didn't ask for any promises,"

he said. "Take off that blouse and lie back down here—" he patted the sand beside him "—and let's discuss it."

She shook her head, still smiling. "We have to catch a kidnapper," she reminded him. "So don't distract me."

"I told you, this is boring," he said. "I'm not used to inactivity."

"Neither am I, but this goes with the job description." She peered up over the dune. The kids were still working on that sand castle, making it more elaborate by the minute. But there was no one in sight, no one at all. The kids had been kept close while Janine got over her concussion and was recovering. Perhaps the kidnappers had given up.

She murmured the thought aloud. Canton lay on his back with his arm shading his eyes from the sun. "Fat chance," he said curtly. "Marie wants her cut of the money and she'll go to any lengths to get it. Karie knows how she is. Poor kid. The last time I went off on business, before the divorce, Marie had one of her lovers upstairs and she was screaming like a banshee with him. When I got home, Karie was sitting on the steps out front in the snow."

She was shocked. "What did you do?"

He sat up, glancing at her. "What would you have done?" he countered.

She shrugged. "I'd have thrown him out the front door as naked as a jaybird and left him to get home the best way he could," she said.

He chuckled. "You and I think alike."

"You didn't!" she exclaimed.

He nodded. "Yes, I did. But I have a more charitable heart than you do. I threw his clothes out after him.''

"And your wife?''

"I think she knew it was all over. She packed and left with a few veiled threats, and something to the effect that she needed other men because I couldn't satisfy her in bed.''

She rolled over and looked up at him. Men were vulnerable there, in their egos, she thought. His eyes were evading hers, but there was pain in the taut lines of his face.

"They say that—''

He cut her off. "Don't start spouting platitudes, for God's sake,'' he muttered. "I don't want any reassurances from a woman who's never had a man in the first place.''

"I was only going to say that I don't think sex matters much unless people love each other. And if they do, it won't really make any difference how good or bad they are at it.''

He shifted, lying on one elbow in the sand. "I wouldn't know. I married Marie because she was outgoing and beautiful, one of the sexiest women I'd ever known. I had money and she wanted it. I thought she wanted me. Life teaches hard lessons. Glitter can blind a man.''

"It can blind anyone. I'm sorry it didn't work out for you.''

"We had ten years together,'' he said. "But only the first few months counted. I had my head stuck in computer programs and she was traveling all over the world to every new fashionable resort for the next nine years. Karie had no family life at all.''

She made an awkward movement and peered over

the dune. The kids were still fine, and nobody was in sight.

"Karie seems happy with you," she said.

"I think she is. I haven't been much of a father in the past. I'm trying to make up for it." He studied her face and smiled gently. "What about you and Kurt? Do your parents care about you?"

She chuckled. "In their way. They're flighty and unworldly and naive. But we take care of them."

He sighed and shook his head. "Parenting is not for the weakhearted."

"I guess not. But kids are sweet. I've always loved having Kurt around."

He pursed his lips and narrowed his eyes and watched her. "Do you want kids of your own?"

"Yes."

He didn't say anything else. He just went on watching her, looking at her with intent curiosity.

"Is my face on crooked?" she murmured, blushing.

He reached up and touched her cheek, very gently. "It's a sweet face," he said solemnly. "Full of concern and mischief and love. I've never known anyone like you. You aren't at all what I thought successful writers were. You're not conceited or condescending. You don't even act like a successful writer."

"I wouldn't have a clue," she replied. "And I'll tell you something. I know a lot of successful writers. They're all nice people."

"Not all of them."

She shrugged. "There are always one or two bad apples in every bunch. But my friends are nice."

"Do they all write mysteries?"

She shook her head. "Some are romance authors, some write science fiction, some write thrillers. We talk over the Internet." She cleared her throat. "Actually a number of us talk about the villain on that science fiction series. We think he's just awesome."

He chuckled. "Lucky for me I look like him, huh?"

She laughed and pushed him. He caught her and rolled over, poised just above her with his face suddenly serious. "That isn't why you're attracted to me, is it?" he asked worriedly.

"I think maybe it was, at first," she admitted.

"And now?"

She bit her lower lip. "Now..."

His thumb moved softly over her mouth, her chin. "Now?"

Her eyes met his and the impact went right through her. Her lips parted. "Oh, glory," she whispered unsteadily.

"Oh, glory," he agreed, bending.

He kissed her in a way he never had before, his mouth barely touching hers, cherishing instead of demanding. His arms were warm but tender, the pressure of his long, powerful body not at all threatening. When he lifted his mouth, hers followed it, her dazed eyes lingering on his lips.

His breathing was as ragged as hers. He touched her face with quiet wonder. It was in his eyes, too, the newness of what he was feeling. He looked odd, hesitant, uncertain.

"I don't have a dime," he said slowly. "Maybe I'll make my fortune back, maybe I won't. You could end up with a computer programmer working for wages."

Her heart jumped. "That sounds like you're talking about something permanent."

He nodded. "Yes."

"You mean...as in living together."

"No."

She blushed. "Sorry, I guess I jumped the gun..."

His fingers pressed against her lips. He struggled for the right words. "It's too soon for big decisions," he said, "but you might start thinking about marriage."

She gasped.

Her reaction hit him right in his pride. Obviously she hadn't even considered a permanent life with him. He cursed and rolled away from her, getting to his feet. He stared out toward the kids, toward the sea, his hands stuck deep in his pockets.

She didn't understand his odd behavior. She got up, too, hesitating.

He glanced at her uneasily. "I'm thirty-eight," he said.

"Yes, I...I know."

"You're twenty-four," he continued. "I suppose your professor is closer to the right age. He's got a degree, too, and he fits in with your family." His eyes went back to the ocean.

She felt a vulnerability in him that made her move closer. "But I don't love him, Canton."

He turned slowly. "I like the way you say my name," he said softly.

She smiled hesitantly. "I like the way you say mine," she replied shyly. Her eyes fell. "Are you sorry you mentioned marriage?"

He moved a step closer. "I thought you were."

Her eyes came up.

"You gasped," he said curtly. "As if it were unthinkable."

"You'd only just said a few days ago that you never wanted to get married again," she explained.

"A man says a lot of things he doesn't mean when a woman's got him tied up in knots," he murmured. "God in heaven, can't you see how it is with me? I want you. But I'm not in your league educational-wise, and I'm flat busted. My wife left me for someone who was better in bed. I'm pushing forty...what are you doing?"

Her hands were busy on the front of his shirt, working at buttons. "Taking your clothes off," she said simply. She looked up with wide green eyes. "Do you mind?"

He didn't seem to be able to speak. His mouth was open.

She pushed the shirt aside, over the expanse of thick hair and hard muscle. He wasn't darkly tanned, but he was sexy. He smelled of spices. She smiled and buried her face in his chest, pressing her lips to it.

He shivered.

She looked up, still caressing him slowly. "You've seen me without any clothes at all, although my head was hurting too much at the time for me to enjoy it. Turnabout is fair play."

"It's a public beach," he noted, barely able to speak.

"You proposed."

"I didn't," he protested huskily. "I said I wanted you to think about it."

Her eyes went back to his chest. He was moving helplessly against the slow caress of her fingers. "I've thought about it."

"And?"

"I like kids." She looked up. "I'd like several. I make a good living writing books. I can take care of the bills until you settle on what you want to do, or while you make your fortune back. I'm good at budgeting, and Karie likes me. I like her, too.''

He couldn't get his breath. "You're driving me mad," he said through his teeth.

Her eyebrows lifted. Her eyes darted to the movement of her hands on his bare chest and back up again to his stormy eyes. "With this?" she asked, fascinated.

His chest rose and fell heavily. His hands covered hers and stilled them. "I've been more concerned with a failing empire and my employees' futures lately to pay much attention to women. It's been a long dry spell," he added. "You understand?"

"Sort of."

"I suppose I'm not the only one who spends too much time at the computer," he mused.

She shifted a little. "I've never found men very attractive physically."

"Oh?"

"Well, until now," she amended. Her searching eyes met his. "I used to dream about traveling. Now I have the most embarrassing dreams about you."

He grinned. "Do tell."

"I wouldn't dare."

"If you'll marry me, we can do something about them."

"I have to marry you first?"

He smiled gently. "My mother was Spanish. She raised me very strictly, in an old-world sort of way. I never messed around with virgins. I'm much too old to start now."

"In other words, good girls get married before they get…"

"I'll wash your mouth out with soap if you say it," he promised.

She wrinkled her nose at him. "I'll bet you'd say it."

"And more," he agreed. "I have a nasty temper."

"I noticed."

"So you know the worst already. And since you aren't experienced, and you have no one to compare me with in bed," he added, tongue-in-cheek, "I'll seem worldly and wise to you." He pursed his lips. "Now, that's an encouraging thought."

She looped her arms around his neck. "I love you," she said softly. "You'll seem like Don Juan to me."

He actually blushed.

"Shouldn't I say that I love you?" she asked.

His arms tightened. "Say it a lot," he instructed. "Karie says it sometimes, but Marie never did. Funny, I never noticed, either." He smiled. "I like the way it sounds."

"You could say it back," she pointed out.

He cleared his throat. "I don't know."

"It's easy." She looked briefly worried. "If you mean it."

"Oh, I mean it, all right," he said, and realized with a start that he did. He hadn't given much thought to the emotional side of his turbulent relationship with her, but the feeling was definitely there. He wanted her, he liked her, he enjoyed being with her. And he most certainly did...love her.

Her eyes had brightened. "You do?"

He nodded. He searched her face quietly. "It's risky, marriage."

"No, it isn't. We'll love each other and take care

of Karie, and Kurt when we need to. We'll have kids and love them and I'll never leave you."

His jaw tautened. His arms closed around her bruisingly, and he held her for a long time without speaking. His tall body shuddered as he felt the full impact of commitment.

She closed her eyes and sighed, moving her soft cheek against the thick hair on his chest. "I like hairy men," she whispered. "It's like holding a teddy bear."

He chuckled, his voice deep at her ear. "Thank God. I'd hate to have to shave my chest every day."

Her arms tightened. "When?" she asked dreamily.

He made the transition without trouble. "Whenever you like," he said. "We have to get rings and arrange a ceremony. It should be easy in Mexico." He lifted his head. "I have a town house in Lincoln Park. I've divided my time between Chicago and New York, but I only have an apartment in New York. I'll try to hold onto it. You might want to go shopping in Manhattan from time to time, or visit your publishers."

She grinned. "You're a prince."

"I'm a pauper," he insisted.

She sighed. "That's okay. I like you better poor. You'll always know that I married you for what you didn't have."

He burst out laughing and lifted her high in his arms. "So I will."

The kids, hearing the commotion, came up the beach to see what all the laughter was about.

"We're going to get married," Canton told them, totally forgetting that he'd only asked Janine to think about marriage. He wasn't about to let her get away.

He watched his daughter's face, and was relieved when he saw it light up.

"You're going to marry Janine? She'll be my step-mom? Cool!" She rushed up and hugged Janine with all her might. "Oh, Janine, that's just the best present I ever got for my birthday!"

"Today's your birthday?" Janine exclaimed. "I didn't know!"

"I got her a cake and a present. We were going to have you both over tonight to celebrate," Canton explained. He grimaced. "I got so wrapped up in what we were talking about, I forgot to mention it."

"I have a neat game program for you," Janine told the girl. "A CD-ROM of Mars. It's a mystery."

"Cool! I love space stuff."

"Yes, I noticed," Janine chuckled. She sighed. "I'm going to love having you for a stepdaughter. But let's leave the step off of it, okay?" she added. "How about Mom and daughter?"

"That suits me," Karie said warmly.

"What about me?" Kurt wailed. "Won't I get to stay with you anymore? I'll be stuck with...*them?*" His voice trailed off as he looked past Janine. "What in the world are they doing here?"

Janine turned, and there were her parents, sweaty and stained with dirt, both wearing khakis and wide-brimmed hats, waving from the deck of the beach house.

"Something must have happened," she said. "Come on." She took Canton by the hand and they all went back down the beach, the stakeout for the would-be kidnappers forgotten for the moment.

The introductions were made quickly. Professors Dan and Joan Curtis were fascinated by Canton

Rourke, whom they'd certainly heard of. To learn that
he was marrying their daughter caused them both to
be momentarily tongue-tied.

"You don't know each other very well," Joan cau-
tioned worriedly.

"We have so much in common that discovering
each other will be a lifelong pleasure," Canton said,
and won her over on the spot.

She grinned at him, looking just like Janine, with
her dark hair and green eyes. Dan was tall and thin
with graying hair and blue eyes. He looked older than
ever as he sat sprawled in a chair sipping cold bottled
water.

In the middle of the living room was a huge crate.
Dan nodded toward it. "That's why we're back."

Janine's eyebrows rose. "Something special?"

"A few good pieces," Dan replied. "We've tried
to contact our man in the Mexican government, but
our satellite link was sabotaged."

"It was what?" Janine exclaimed. "I knew there
had been problems, but I hadn't realized the extent."

"We've had a pothunter on our tails," Dan replied.
"A very determined one. He shot at us."

Janine sat down, with Canton right behind her, his
hand on her shoulder.

"We're all right," Joan said. "But we thought it
would be wise to get back to civilization as quickly
as possible. We jumped into the Land Rover, with
that—" he indicated the crate "—and drove back at
top speed. We lost our guide on the way. He was
behind us in his truck, but we didn't see him again.
We phoned the police the minute we got in. They
should be along momentarily."

"If there's anything I can do, I'll be glad to help," Canton volunteered.

"He got us in touch with you," Janine added helpfully. "He knows the president of the country personally."

The Curtises were impressed. They both stared at Canton with renewed interest.

"Would the pothunters try anything here in Cancún?" Janine asked worriedly.

"For what's in that box, they would," Dan said mournfully. "In a way, I'm sorry we found such a brilliant site. We've mapped everything, taken photos, documented every step of the excavation so that nothing was overlooked. That will help future expeditions in their excavations."

"Won't the government send someone to take possession of these pieces?" Janine asked.

"Certainly," Joan replied with a smile. "It's just a matter of getting them down here. And keeping the pothunters away until they can."

Dan Curtis took a pistol from his pocket and put it on the table. "This business is getting to be very dangerous."

"Archaeology always was," Janine said pointedly. "Even in the early days. But it's worthwhile."

"We always thought so, didn't we, dear?" Joan asked her husband, with a loving hand on his shoulder.

His hand went up to take hers. "We still do. But we're getting old for this."

Dan stared at the crate again. "I hope that isn't going to get any of us hurt. We almost checked into a hotel instead of coming here, but this seemed wiser."

"It is," Canton said firmly. "I've got a man watching my beach house. He can get another man to help him and watch this one, too.''

Joan frowned. ''Why do you have someone watching it?''

''Because my mom tried to have me kidnapped,'' Karie explained. ''Janine got kidnapped instead and hit on the head and was in the hospital...''

''What?'' Joan and Dan exclaimed together.

''I'm fine,'' Janine said gently, holding up a hand. ''I haven't forgotten any of my training.''

''You and detective work,'' Joan moaned. ''Darling, archaeology would have been so much safer!''

''Ha! You're the ones who got shot at, remember?'' Janine replied. ''Anyway, we saved Karie from kidnappers, but we're not sure that they've given up. It's been sort of hectic around here for the past week.''

''And here we come with more trouble,'' Dan groaned.

Janine patted him on the shoulder. ''It's okay, Dad. There are enough of us to guard the crate and Karie. We'll be fine.''

''Of course we will,'' Canton agreed.

Dan and Joan exchanged wan smiles, but they didn't look convinced.

''Just out of idle curiosity, what have you got in the box?'' Janine asked.

''Several Mayan funerary statues, some pottery, a few tablets with glyphs on them and some gold jewelry with precious stones inlaid. Oh, and a jeweled funeral mask.''

Janine's eyes widened. ''A king's ransom,'' she said.

''And all the property of the Mexican government, as soon as we can turn it over,'' Dan added. ''We're hoping to keep at least one or two of the pots for our own collection at the university, but that's up to the powers-that-be.''

"Considering what you've gone through to get it, I imagine they won't begrudge you a piece or two," Canton said. He moved forward. "It's been nice to meet you. I have to get Karie home and make a couple of business calls. We'll see you later.''

"I'll walk out with you," Janine said after the Curtises had made their goodbyes.

Karie went ahead of them. Canton slid his arm around Janine's shoulders and held her close. "Complications," he murmured.

"More and more. Maybe the kidnappers will back off, with so many people around."

"Maybe they'll join forces with the pothunters," he murmured.

She poked him in the side with her elbow. "Stop being pessimistic. This is all going to work out. It has to, and soon. I want to get married."

"What a coincidence, so do I!" he murmured facetiously.

She laughed, turning her face up to his. "The sooner the better," she added.

He nodded. "The sooner, the better." He bent and kissed her gently. "Go home."

"Be careful."

"You, too. I'll phone you later. Lock your doors. I'm going to make a few telephone calls and see what I can do to help things along."

"Have your ex-wife arrested," she suggested.

"Nice sentiment, but not practical." He chuckled.

"All the same, there may be some way to discourage her. I'll find one." He winked. "Stay out of trouble."

"You do the same."

Chapter Ten

"I can't believe this," Joan Curtis said heavily. "My daughter is marrying Mr. Software. Do you have any idea how famous he is, how much money he's made in his life?"

"He's broke right now," Janine stated.

"He'll never be broke, not with a mind like his," Dan said with a grin. "He's one smart guy. He'll make it all back, with interest."

"Even if he doesn't, it won't matter. I'm crazy about him," Janine confessed.

"It seems to be mutual. And here I thought you were going to wait around forever for Quentin to propose," Joan teased. "I'm glad that never happened, Janine," she added. "Quentin was never the man for you."

"I know that, now. I just drifted along until I met Canton."

"Listen," Joan called suddenly, her eyes on the

television. "They're tracking a hurricane. They say it's coming this way!"

"A hurricane?" Dan groaned. "Just what we need!" He glanced at his daughter. "You didn't mention this."

"I didn't know," she said. "I don't speak Spanish!"

"It's in English now," Joan observed.

Janine looked sheepish. "Well, I've been rather out of things for several days, and I haven't been watching television."

"No wonder," Dan mused.

"You must have noticed the wind picking up, and the clouds," Joan said, sighing. "They've just said that they may have to evacuate the coast if it comes any closer. And it looks as if it's going to."

"I had hoped to get a plane back to the States," Dan said, glancing worriedly at the crate. "Now what do we do?"

"We go further inland," Janine said at once. "Canton has a rental car. We need a van, so that we can take your cargo with us."

"With pothunters and potential kidnappers two steps behind." Dan Curtis sighed. "Remember the old days in graduate school, when the most dangerous thing we did was set off a cherry bomb in the dean's car?"

"You what?" Janine exclaimed, grinning.

Dan grinned and exchanged a look with his wife. "We weren't always old," he murmured.

"No time for reminiscing," Joan said, and she was picking up things as she went. "Get cracking. We have to pack up and get out of here, quick."

Before she had a case packed, Canton and the kids were back.

"Hurricane Opal is headed our way," he began, noticing the disorder in the living room.

"We know," Janine said. "We're packing up to go inland. We need to rent a van."

"Leave that to me. There's safety in numbers. We'll go together. I have a friend who owns an estate halfway between here and Chichén Itzá. He'll be able to have us stay. And he has armed security," he added with a chuckle.

"Armed security?" Janine was intrigued.

"He was a mercenary in his younger days. Now he's a married man with two kids. They moved down here from Chicago because of the tough winters. Not much snow in Quintana Roo," he added merrily.

"What interesting people you know, Mr. Rourke," Dan remarked.

"Call me Canton. Yes, I do have some unique acquaintances. I'll see about that van. Karie, you stay here with Kurt and Janine."

"Oh, Dad, does he have a TV?" she asked worriedly. "I have to watch the Braves game. It's the playoffs!"

"They're never going to win the series," he began.

She stuck out her lower lip. "Yes, they are! I believe in them!"

He just shook his head.

Two hours later, they were fighting headwinds and rain as they plowed down the long narrow paved road toward the estate of Canton's friends.

The jungle was on either side of them. They saw small *pueblos* nestled among the trees, many with satellite dishes and electricity. Advertising signs were nailed to trees and even the sides of small wooden buildings here and there. There were huge speedbreakers at the beginning and end of each little town they passed.

Down the dusty streets, children played in the rain and dogs barked playfully. As they went past the small, neat houses, they could see hammocks nestled against the walls, ready to be slung again each night. The floors of the whitewashed houses, though earthen, were unlittered and smooth. Tiny stores sat among unfamiliar trees, and in several places, religious shrines were placed just off the road.

Two tour buses went by them. The buses were probably bound for ancient Mayan cities like Chichén Itzá. Janine and Kurt had been on one during their first week in Cancún. The large vehicles were surprisingly comfortable, and the tour guides were walking encyclopedias of facts about present and past in the Yucatán.

"You're very quiet," Joan remarked from the front seat of the van. "Would you rather have gone with the Rourkes?"

"They've got Kurt," she said. "I thought I might need to stay with you."

Dan chuckled. "Protecting us, is that it?"

She only smiled. "Well, neither of you know any martial arts."

"That's true, darling." Joan touched her hand gently. "Whatever would we do without you?"

"I have no idea," Janine said dryly, and meant it, although they didn't suspect that.

The estate of Canton's friend had two men with rifles at the black wrought-iron gates. Whatever Canton said to them produced big smiles. The gate opened, and Canton's arm out the window motioned the van to follow.

The house had arches. It was snowy white with a red tile roof, and blooming flowers everywhere. It looked Spanish, and right at home in the jungle.

As they reached the front porch, wide and elegant with a few chairs scattered about and a huge hammock, the front door opened and two people came out.

The man was tall, dark, very elegant. He had a mustache and looked very Latin. The woman was smaller, with long blond hair and a baby in her arms. A little boy of about nine came out the door behind them.

When the vehicles stopped, the Curtises got out and joined the Rourkes and Kurt.

The dark man came forward. "You made good time," he told Canton, and they shook hands warmly. "These are the Curtises of whom you spoke? *Bienvenidos a mi casa,*" he said. "Welcome to my home. I am Diego Laremos. This is my wife, Melissa, our son Matt, and our baby daughter, Carmina." He turned and spoke softly to the blond woman. "*Enamorada,* this is Canton Rourke, of whom you have heard me speak."

"I'm delighted to meet you," the woman spoke with a smile and a faint British accent. "Diego and I are happy to have you stay with us. Believe me, you're all quite safe here."

"Many thanks for putting us up," Dan Curtis said, extending a hand. "We have some priceless things that pothunters have been trying their best to steal. We had hoped to fly to the States today, but they were evacuating Cancún."

"So Canton told me," Diego replied solemnly.

"Pothunters are ever a problem. So it was in Guatemala, where Melissa and I lived."

"We tried to live in Chicago, but the winters were too harsh," Melissa said with a rueful smile. "We were nervous about taking Matt to Guatemala, so we eventually moved here. Isn't it beautiful?"

"Absolutely," Janine said. "It must be wonderful to live year-round in such a paradise."

Canton put an arm around her. "Think so?" he asked gently. "Then I'll see about buying some land nearby, if you like it."

"Could we?" Janine exclaimed. "How wonderful. We could visit Melissa."

Melissa beamed. "Yes, you could. I have all your books," she added sheepishly.

"Now that really makes me feel welcome. May I hold him?" she asked, moving toward the baby with bright, intrigued eyes.

"Her." Melissa corrected her with a chuckle. "Indeed you may." Melissa handed the baby over, and Janine cradled her warmly, her whole face radiant as the tiny little girl looked at her with dark blue eyes and began to coo.

"Oh, what a darling!" she exclaimed, breathless.

Canton, watching her, had an incredible mental picture of how Janine would look holding their own baby, and he caught his breath.

She looked up, into his eyes, smiling shyly. "Can we have several of these?"

"As many as you like," he replied huskily.

"I'll take you up on that," she promised.

The Laremoses were the most interesting people Janine had met, and she'd met a lot. Diego had two other ex-mercenary friends in Chicago, one who'd practiced law there for years and was now an appellate court judge, and another who ran a top secret security school of some sort. Both were married and had families.

"There's another member of the old group in Texas," he added. "He's married, too, and they have a ranch. And then there's one who lives in Montana. He got fed up with the city and took his wife and kids out there. They have a ranch, too. We have reunions every year, but with all the kids involved, we have to have them in the summer."

"They're a unique bunch," Canton said musingly. "And all ex-mercenaries. I'm amazed that you all lived to marry and have families in the first place."

Laremos leaned forward. "So were we."

Canton smiled at Janine over the huge dinner table, where they were eating salads and drinking fine, rich coffee. "I met this bunch at a time in my life when I was having some extreme problems with a small hardware enterprise I'd set up in a Third World country. Mine was ecologically friendly, but there was a rival company tearing up the rain forest and killing off the natives. When the government said that it didn't have the money or manpower to do anything about the situation, I sent Laremos and his group over and they arranged a few unpleasant, but nonlethal, surprises for them. They packed up and left."

"Good for you," Janine said with admiration.

"We also set up a trust and bought land for the tribe, which is theirs forever. I don't like profit with a bedrock of destruction," Canton said simply. "I never did."

"I hope you get it all back, *amigo*," Laremos said sincerely. "We need more industrialists like you, men who balance profit with compassion for the environment.''

"Profit is the last thing on my mind right now," Canton said, leaning back. "I hope that we can discourage the people who are after us. I think we were followed coming down here."

"No doubt you were. But," Laremos said with a grin, "your pursuers are in for a great surprise if they attempt to come here. My men are dedicated and antisocial. And armed."

"We noticed," Janine said. Her eyes twinkled. "I'm already getting ideas for another book."

"Are you going to put us in it?" Melissa asked, bright-eyed. "I want to be a blond, sexy siren who entices this big, strong Latino and makes him wild."

"You do that every day of my life, *enamorada*," Diego said, bringing her soft hand to his mouth. "No need to tell the world about it."

She only smiled. A look passed between them that made Janine smile, too. It must be wonderful to be married so long, and still be in love. Her gaze went to Canton, and found him watching her.

He didn't say a word. But his eyes told her that she and he would be that happy, for that long. In fact, his smile promised it.

They had to stay for two days at the estate before the storm was on its way. Before it finally became disorganized, it left major damage along its path.

There had been no sign of the would-be kidnappers or the pothunters, but when the Curtises and the Rourkes left the elegant Laremos estate, it was to find themselves once again being trailed. And this time, there were two vehicles in pursuit and they didn't bother to hang back.

The Rourke car and the van in which the Curtises were riding raced past small villages, only slowing for the speedbreakers. Still the two cars gained on them. They came to a crossroads, and Canton suddenly motioned to Dan Curtis to follow him. He took the right fork at speed and then suddenly whipped the car off onto a little dirt trail into some trees, motioning out the window for Dan to follow.

The tree cover was thick and the rain had removed the problem of telltale dust rising to give away their positions.

He cut off his engine. Dan did likewise. Then they sat and waited. Only seconds later, the two pursuing cars slowed, stopped, looked around. They pulled up beside each other on the narrow little paved road and spoke rapidly, after which each car took a fork and raced away.

Canton reversed the car until it was even with the van. "We can return to the last village and cut through there back to the Cancún road. Don't lose your nerve."

"Not me," Dan said with a grin. "Lead on."

"Are you okay?" he asked Janine, who was once again with her parents.

She nodded. "I'm fine. Take care of Kurt and Karie."

"You know I will."

He waved and raced away, with the van right behind. They managed to get enough of a head start to lose the pursuing vehicles, but they were not out of danger. The occupants of the car would soon realize that they'd been outfoxed and turn around.

By the time the pursuers got back into the village,
though, the people they were chasing were long gone.
Of course, there was only one road, and they'd surely
know to backtrack on it. But at the last *pueblo* there
had been a turnoff to Cancún that had two forks. One
of them led north, the other east. The pursuers would
be obliged to split up. And even if one car took the
right fork, there wouldn't be any way they could catch
up in time. Janine thought admiringly that her future
husband would make a dandy detective.

They arrived in Cancún after dark and checked into
a hotel, having decided that the beach house would be
much too dangerous. They unloaded the car and the
van, which were then returned to the rental agencies
and another, different van was rented from still another
agency. Janine thought it might be possible to throw
the pursuers off the track this way.

And it might have been; except that the would-be
kidnappers spotted Canton with Janine at the car rental
lot and immediately realized what was going on. They
didn't follow the van back to the hotel. One of the
local men had a cousin who was friendly with an em-
ployee at the car rental agency. All she had to do was
flirt a little with the agent. Within an hour, they knew
not only which hotel, but which rooms, contained their
prey.

To make matters worse, the pothunter, also a local
man, had family connections to one of the people who
were after Karie. They decided to pool their resources
and split the profits.

With no suspicion of all this, Canton and Janine and
the others settled into adjoining rooms of the hotel
while they waited to get on the next flight to Chicago.

Karie had discovered that there was no way she was going to get any telecast of a Braves game now, with communications affected by the hurricane. Power lines and communications cables had been downed and service was interrupted. As she told her dad, they might not have a tropical beach in Chicago, but they did have cable.

The Curtises were ready to go home as well. Their weeks of grubbing in the outer reaches of Quintana Roo had paid great dividends. They not only had plenty to show the Mexican government, but they also had enough research material for a book and several years of lectures.

A representative of the government was going to meet them early in the morning in the hotel and go over the crated artifacts with them.

Little did they know, however, that the representative had been waylaid and replaced by a henchman of the pothunters....

"It's going to be a great relief to have these treasures off our hands," Dan Curtis remarked over dinner that evening. "Not that I'm sorry we found them, but they're quite a responsibility."

"Did you know that in the early part of this century, archaeologists went to Chichén Itzá to look for artifacts and were murdered there?" Joan added.

"I was watching a program on that on the Discovery Channel," Janine remarked. "It was really interesting. After the first archaeologists went there, the Peabody Museum of Harvard had an agent in Mexico gathering material for them in the early part of the century. It's in drawers in the museum and isn't on display to the public. But it belongs to Mexico. So why doesn't the Mexican government ask them to give it back? In fact, there are human skeletal remains in that collection as well, aren't there? Certainly with all the new laws governing such remains, they should be reinterred, shouldn't they?"

"Those laws don't apply universally," Dan Curtis ventured. "And there probably would be something like a grandfather clause even if they did. That particular collection dates to the time before the Mexican Revolution, long before there were such laws." He smiled gently. "It's more complicated than it seems to a lay person. But believe me, archaeology has come a long way in the past few decades."

"Just the same, it's a pity, isn't it?" Janine added. "I mean, nobody gets to see the exquisite Maya artwork in the collection, least of all the descendants of the Mayan people in Quintana Roo."

"But they're also preserved for future generations," Dan explained. "Artifacts left in situ are very often looted and sold on the black market, ending up with collectors who don't dare show them to anyone." He smiled at his daughter. "I know it's not a perfect system," he mused, "but right now, it's the best we can do."

"Yes, I know. There are two sides to every story. You both take your work seriously. And you do it very well," Janine said with a smile, because she was proud of her parents. They cared about their work. They were never slipshod in their excavations or disrespectful of the human skeletal remains they frequently unearthed.

"I do wish we'd had a little more time," Dan said ruefully. "I think we were onto something. We found an unusual ceremonial site, unlike anything we've discovered before. We were just beginning to unearth it when the trouble started.''

"A superstitious mind would immediately think of curses," Janine said wickedly.

Dan chuckled, winking at his wife. "Trust a writer to come up with something like that. No, there's no curse, just bad luck. Señor Perez has been following us ever since we got off the plane. He tried bribery at first, and when that didn't work he began making veiled threats about intervention by the Mexican government. We had all the necessary permits and permissions, so the threats didn't work, either. Then he set up camp nearby and began harassing us."

"Harassing? How?" Janine asked, noting that Canton was listening attentively.

"Sudden noises in the middle of the night. Missing supplies. Stolen tools. There wasn't anything we could specifically charge him with. We couldn't even prove he was at the site, although we knew it was him." Dan shook his head. "Finally it was too much for us, especially after we lost the satellite link. We took what we had and left."

"But what about the site now?" Canton asked somberly. "Won't he loot it?"

"He thinks we have everything that was there, that's the funny part," Joan said. "We were so cautious about the newest find that we didn't even let the workers near it. We concealed it and marked the location on our personal maps. We'll make sure those get into the right hands. Meanwhile," she added heavily, "we've got to get the artifacts we recovered into the right hands, before Señor Perez can trace us here and do something drastic."

"Would he?" Janine asked worriedly.

Dan nodded. "An expedition lost a member along with some priceless gold and jeweled artifacts some years ago. Perez was implicated but there wasn't enough evidence for him to be prosecuted. He always hires henchmen to do his dirty work."

Janine felt chilled. She wrapped her arms around herself, glad that Kurt and Karie were on the patio and not listening to this.

"I have my man and another watching the hotel," Canton said. "We'll be safe enough here until we can get a plane out."

Karie and Kurt had left the balcony and had gone into Kurt's room. They came out with a rather large bag.

"Could we go down to the beach for just a minute?" Karie asked, with her camera slung around her neck. "We want to snap some photographs."

"I don't think that's a good idea," Canton said.

"Aw, please, Dad," Karie moaned. "It's safe here, you said so. There are people looking out for us. Mom won't try again."

Karie took off her Atlanta Braves baseball cap and wiped her sweaty blond hair. "Please?"

They looked desperate. It was hard for kids to be cooped up all day.

"All right. Let me make a phone call first," Canton said. "And make sure Kurt's parents don't mind."

"It's okay, if they'll be watched," Dan agreed.

They exchanged conspiratorial glances. "Thanks, Dad!" Karie said enthusiastically.

Canton made his phone call. The kids took their bag and went down the steps to the ground floor, and out toward the white beach.

"Stay out of the ocean!" Canton called after them.

"Sure, Dad!" Karie agreed.

"What have they got in that bag?" Janine asked curiously.

"They're probably going to collect seashells in it," Canton murmured, sliding an arm around her. He smiled. "Don't worry. I'll make sure they don't bring anything alive back with them."

Janine shuddered delicately. "You're sure your man will watch them?"

He nodded. "He's one of the best in the business. When he isn't working for me, he works for the federal government."

"Oh? As what?"

He chuckled. "I don't know. He says it's classified. He travels a lot." He glanced down at her and smiled. "But he's good. Very good. The kids will be safe."

"Okay."

Kurt glanced over his shoulder as he and Karie rushed down to the sand near the water. "Whew," he said, wiping his brow. "I never thought they'd let us out of the room! And we've gone to all this trouble to get things together, too!"

"I know," Karie said, equally relieved. "And they didn't even ask about the bag, thank goodness."

"We'd better get busy," he said. "We don't have much time."

"Stupid kidnappers and pothunters," she muttered as she unzipped the bag. "They sure know how to make life hard on enterprising preteens, don't they?"

Chapter Eleven

The kids played on the beach. Dan and Joan Curtis rummaged through their crate of artifacts, double-checking everything in preparation for the arrival of the government antiquities representative.

Meanwhile, Canton and Janine sat on the balcony, holding hands. They were too nervous to let Kurt and Karie completely out of sight.

"What are they doing?" Janine asked, frowning as she watched the bag being slowly unpacked.

"Maybe they've got some cups and glasses to use in sand castle sculpting," he suggested. "Karie always empties the china cupboard when she's planning one."

"Could be," she murmured. But that didn't look like cups and glasses. It looked like pieces of hose, a cow skull, some pieces of rubber, a bag of feathers, several small balloons and a little fur. "Look at all that stuff," she exclaimed. "Could they be making a sand castle with it?"

He let go of her hand and moved closer to the balcony. His eyebrows lifted. "Strange sort of a sand castle…"

The sudden shrill of the telephone caught their attention. Inside the room, Dan Curtis picked up the receiver and began conversing with someone.

"Yes, I could," Dan said slowly, and Janine knew from the past that he was deliberating when he spoke like that. "But why?"

There was a pause.

"I see. But it's a lot of work to pack it all up again," Dan explained. "Why can't you come to the hotel?"

Canton, interested now, got up and went into the room. "Who is it?" he mouthed at Dan.

Dan put his hand over the receiver. "The man from the ministry of antiquities."

"What's his name?" he asked shortly.

"What's your name?" Dan asked the man.

"Carlos Ramirez" came the reply.

Dan relayed it to Canton.

Canton nodded. His eyes narrowed. "Now ask him how Lupe likes her eggs cooked."

It was an odd request, but Dan passed it on. Seconds passed and suddenly the connection was cut.

"Ha!" Canton burst out with a satisfied smile.

"You sound just like him," Janine sighed dreamily.

He scowled. "Just like whom?"

She flushed. "Never mind."

Canton threw up his hands. "I am not an alien," he said. "Neither am I an actor!"

"Sorry," she said, wincing.

He glared at her. "Later, we have to talk." He turned back to Dan. "What did he want you to do?"

"He wanted me to crate up all the artifacts and

drive them into town, to a government warehouse, he said.''

"More likely into a trap," Canton replied angrily. "They must realize that we have this place staked out. They tried to trick you. It didn't work. They won't stop there."

"What will they do now?" Joan asked worriedly.

"I don't know" came the quiet reply. "But the first step would be to put a call through to the real minister of antiquities," he added. "And I can do that for you, right now."

He picked up the telephone and made a long-distance call to Mexico City and asked for the official by name when he was connected with the governmental offices.

There was a greeting and a rapid-fire exchange of greetings and questions. Janine heard the name Lupe mentioned.

"Lupe is the minister's wife," Joan translated. She chuckled as she listened to the conversation. "And she doesn't eat eggs—she's allergic to them."

Another question and a pause and still another, then a quick thank you and Canton hung up.

"He's sending some men right down," Canton said. "And they'll not only have proper identification, they'll have guns. If the pothunter has tapped into this telephone line, he got an earful."

Janine listened interestedly, and then suddenly realized that they'd left Karie and Kurt on the beach and weren't watching them.

She turned and ran out onto the balcony, scanned the beach, and her heart stopped. The kids were nowhere in sight. There was a long, odd mound of sand where they'd been, but no kids.

"They're gone!" she cried.

Canton and Dan were halfway out the door before she finished, leaving her to follow and Joan to stay behind and watch the crate.

They took the stairs to the ground floor instead of the elevator and ran toward the beach, automatically splitting up as they reached the back of the hotel. Dan went one way, Canton and Janine the other.

A loud cry alerted them. It came from the shadowy confines of the unoccupied wooden scuba rental station.

Two men had Karie and Kurt and two others were rushing toward them. One had a gun.

"Oh, my God, it's him!" Janine blurted out when she got a good look at the man with the gun. "It's the kidnapper and his cohorts!"

"That's Perez, the pothunter, who has Kurt," Dan Curtis said furiously. "For God's sake, they've joined forces," he groaned. His voice carried as he glared toward them. "Let go of those kids, you slimy cowards!" he raged at the men.

The two men holding Karie and Kurt moved out into the sunlight, the man with the exposed pistol by their side. Janine sank a little lower into the sand, thinking. She didn't dare rush the man with the gun, but if there was any opening at all she was going to take it.

"Don't," Canton said under his breath as he saw her tense and sensed what she was thinking. "For God's sake, you have to trust me, this once. I have an ace in the hole. Give me a chance to play it!"

Dan, standing beside his daughter, didn't understand. Neither did Janine. But Canton's deep voice held such conviction, such certainty, that they hesitated. He wouldn't risk Karie. He must have a trade in mind, a bargain of some sort. Wheeling and dealing was his stock in trade. If there was an angle, he'd know it.

Janine waited with bated breath, hardly daring to look at the frightened faces of the children as they were held securely by the two men.

"We want the Mayan treasure, Señor Curtis," the man, Perez, demanded. "We want it now. If you give it to us, we will let the children go. Otherwise, we will take them with us until you comply with our... request."

"Joined forces, have you?" Canton drawled. "How convenient."

"There is an advantage in superior numbers," Perez said smoothly. "I required assistance and these men only want to be paid off. They have no further wish to work for Señor Rourke's former wife, who has not even paid them for their services to date."

"Typical of Marie," Canton replied. "They should have known better. And so should you. You crossed the line this time. And you'll pay with a very long prison sentence."

"We have the gun, *señor*," Perez said with a mocking smile.

"Do you really?" Canton nodded toward the familiar tall, dark man with the gun, who turned with an action so smooth and quick that Janine barely saw him move as he freed Karie and Kurt from the grasps of their captors, leaving both men groaning and shivering on the sand. Perez backed away with his hands in a supplicating position. The gun was trained on him now, and the attacker hardly looked mussed.

Janine's gasp was audible as Dan held out his arms

to Kurt and Canton did the same to a frightened, weeping Karie.

"For scaring the children so, I really should finish them off," the tall, dark man said without expression as he looked from Perez to the still writhing men on the ground. The pistol hadn't wavered once. Perez swallowed audibly.

"It is a misunderstanding," he faltered.

"Yours," the dark man agreed. His eyes cut back to Canton. "Well?"

"The Mexican authorities can deal with them," Canton said coldly. "And the more harshly, the better. Kidnapping is a cowardly act. If he'd hurt my daughter, I'd have killed him."

"I was close by," the dark man replied. "And so was my colleague." He waved to a man down the beach, who turned and went away. "There was never a minute when the children were in any real danger, I assure you." His black eyes slid over Perez's pale face. "I could have dropped him at any time."

"I think he realizes that. Thanks for your help, Rodrigo."

He shrugged. "*De nada.* I owed you a favor." He nodded, motioning for Perez and the other two men, who were on their feet if shaken, to go ahead of him.

"But he pushed me off the boat," Janine said insistently. "Didn't you hear what I told you about him?"

"He infiltrated the kidnapping gang," Canton told her. "I didn't dare tell you who he was. One slip could have cost him his life. Not that he's ever been shy about risking it for a good cause," he added. He looked down at Karie. "Are you okay, pumpkin?"

"Yes, Dad. *Wasn't it exciting?*" she burst out.

"It sure was! He had a gun, too! Where's Mom?" Kurt added, looking around. "I've got to go tell her!"

"Make her sit down first," Dan called.

Karie took off with him, and Janine wondered all over again at the resilience of the very young. She just shook her head.

"No wonder he was always hanging around," she said. "I should have my detective's license pulled for being so blind."

"He's good at his job."

"Tell me about it." She glanced at him. "Is he CIA?"

He smiled. "I don't know. I told you, I've never been clear about the agency he works for. When I knew him, he, like Laremos and the others, was a mercenary. He was with them in Africa."

She pursed her lips. "A book is forming in my mind…" she began.

"Have Señor Perez eaten by giant alligators," Dan suggested to her. "On second thought, quicksand is a nice touch."

"Prison sounds much better, don't you think?" she countered. "Don't worry, I'll take care of that little detail." She looked up at Canton. "Will she try again?" she asked worriedly.

"Who, Marie?" He shrugged. "I doubt it. She's basically lazy, and when she realizes that she may be implicated in the gutter press in an international kidnapping story, that will probably be enough to stifle any future ambitions. She'll have to wait for her alimony."

"How can she get alimony when she's remarried?" Janine wanted to know.

"She calls it child support."

"You have the child," she said pointedly.

He chuckled. "True."

"You need a good attorney."

"I suppose so." He caught her hand warmly in his. "And a minister."

She smiled gently. "Oh, yes. And a minister."

Dan slipped away while they were staring at each other, thinking privately that they were going to be a good match. Canton and Janine had a lot in common, not the least of which was their penchant for surprises. He was overwhelmed that the pothunter was finally going to be out of circulation.

He went back into the hotel room to find a pale Joan being regaled with gory summations of the incident by the two children.

"Don't believe anything they told you," Dan told her comfortingly. "It's all lies."

"Aw, Dad," Kurt groaned. "We were building her up."

"Let her down," he suggested. "It's all over now."

"Or it will be," Joan said, sighing, "when the government official gets here to take the artifacts back to Mexico City."

"The guy that Janine attacked was a spy, and he was working for Karie's dad," Kurt told his mother. "You should have seen him deck those guys. Gosh, it was like watching that spy movie we just saw—"

"Except that it was real," Karie added. She glanced at her watch. "The game's already started," she groaned. "I won't even get to see if my team makes it to the World Series!"

"The airport will be back on schedule by tomorrow, I'm sure, and we can all go home," Dan Curtis said with relief. "I can't say I'll be sorry, this time."

"Nor I," Joan agreed. She hugged Kurt. "One way or another, it's been a hard few weeks. Where are the other two?" she asked suddenly, looking around.

"Down on the beach staring at each other."

"They'll get over that in about thirty years," Dan mused.

Joan grinned at him. "Think so? Then we have ten to go."

"At least."

Canton was walking back toward the hotel with Janine's hand in his, but he looked preoccupied and aloof. She knew that something was worrying him, but she didn't know what.

"Are you absolutely sure that it isn't my resemblance to your science fiction hero that made you agree to marry me?" he asked.

So that was it. She was relieved. Her fingers curled into his big ones. "Yes, I'm sure," she told him. "I've already said so."

"So you have. But you keep coming up with these little comparisons. It's worrying."

"I'm sorry," she said genuinely, stopping to look up at him. "I won't do it again."

He sighed, searching her eyes quietly. "I've been thinking about getting married."

She could see it coming, as if she sensed a hesitation in him. "You don't want to?"

His eyes were troubled. "I want to. But not yet."

Her heart felt as if it were breaking. She smiled in spite of it. "Okay."

"Just like that?"

"Never let it be said that I trapped a man into marriage," she said airily, turning her pained eyes away,

so that he couldn't see them. "I've got a deadline that
I have to meet right now, so it would be more convenient for me, too, if we put our plans on the back
burner and let them simmer for a while."

He shoved his hands into his pockets. "Then let's
do that. I'll give you a call in a month or so and we'll
see where we stand."

"Fine," she agreed.

They parted company at the front door, all the excitement over for the moment. Janine put on a brave
face for her family all evening and then cried herself
to sleep. The one kind thing was that nobody had
asked any questions. She couldn't know that her
pinched, white face told them all they needed to know.
The next day, the government official arrived and took
charge of the artifacts. Shortly thereafter, the Curtises
boarded a plane for Indiana and Janine flew to Chicago. Canton and Karie had elected to stay another
few days in Cancún, so they'd said their goodbyes at
the beach house. It had wounded Janine that Canton
didn't even shake hands. He smiled very pleasantly
and wished them a good trip home, promising to be
in touch. And that was it.

It turned out not to be one month, but two, before
she heard from Canton again. In that length of time,
the Atlanta Braves won the World Series in an incredible game that went all the way to the eighth in-
ning with no score until a home run by the Braves
ended the deadlock. The other team couldn't catch up,
although they tried valiantly. Kurt had a call from an
almost hysterically happy Karie, who sent him a
Braves cap and a World Series victory T-shirt by over-
night mail. From Canton, there was no word. Even

Karie didn't mention him in her telephone call. Apparently her mother had stopped pursuing either her or her father, and that was good news.

Janine, meanwhile, finished her book and started on a new one, set in Cancún. She went back to watching her favorite television program, groaning at the continued absence of her alien villain until news of his reappearance surfaced through the internet fan club to give her a reason for celebration. She watched him in one rerun and on tape, and it occurred to her that even though he resembled Canton, the resemblance wasn't strong enough to account for her ongoing attraction to the missing tycoon. She wondered what he was doing and where he was. His movements lately seemed a mystery to everyone, including the media, which was now joyfully following him again.

The only tidbit of news came through a tabloid, which pictured him with a ravishing brunette at some elegant party. She was looking up at him with bright eyes, and he was smiling down at her. So much for hope, Janine thought as she shredded the picture in the paper and smushed it into the trash can. The heartless philanderer!

She went back to work with a sore heart, not even roused by the forthcoming holiday season. Christmas decorations were up now in Chicago, the television schedule was scattered with reruns of regular programs and holiday specials. Janine worked right through them.

Her parents and Kurt had put up a Christmas tree. Quentin called to say hello and mentioned that he was having the occasional date with the English major he'd met on his trip. He spoke of her with such warmth that Janine was certain that education was not the only thing the two of them discussed. She was happy for him. She and Quentin could never have lived together.

"Hey, isn't this one for the books!" Kurt exclaimed. "Take a look!"

He handed Janine a financial magazine. Inside there was a story about a successful merger of a software company with a hardware computer firm, and there was a photo of Canton Rourke shaking hands with a well-known Texan who owned a line of expensive computers.

"They say he'll make back every penny he's lost, and more," Kurt read. He glanced wickedly at Janine. "I told you he would."

She looked away. "So you did. More power to him."

"Doesn't it matter to you?"

She turned back with a poker face. "Why should it?" she asked. "He hasn't even phoned in two months. I'm sure he wrote me off as a holiday flirtation, and why not? He can have the most beautiful women in the world. What would he want with me?"

Kurt was taken aback. Janine was a dish. She didn't seem aware of it, but Kurt was certain that Canton Rourke had found her irresistible. Karie had said as much, when they were in Cancún. Of course, Janine was right, he hadn't even called since their return to Chicago. That really was too bad. He'd have thought they were made for each other.

He wanted to say something to comfort her, but Janine was already buried in her book again. With a sigh, he went on about his business.

Idly he wondered what Karie had done with the photographs they'd taken in Cancún. Every day, he'd expected to hear something momentous from her about them. She had contacts, she'd said, and she was bound to find someone who'd be ecstatic about them. But to date, he hadn't heard a word. Perhaps she'd given up on the idea in the fervor of having the Braves win the pennant. Or maybe her dad had gotten wind of their secret project and confiscated the photos. Either way, he thought he'd heard the last of it....

Two days later, a tabloid's front page showed a "sea monster" washed up on the beach at Cancún, of all places! It had fur and feathers and gruesome green skin. Its skull resembled most closely that of a bovine. Scientists said it was a new form of life.

Kurt bought three copies and ran back from the corner newsstand to the house he shared with his parents. Janine was visiting over the weekend. Kurt waved the headline under Janine's nose, disrupting one of her best new scenes on her laptop computer. "Look!" he exclaimed. "Just look! It was found right on the beach where we were!"

She looked at the creature with a frown. Something was nagging at the back of her mind when she saw the blown-up photo of the "creature."

Before she could really have time to think about it, there was a knock at the front door.

"See who that is while I save my file, could you?" she asked Kurt, putting the tabloid aside. "Look through the peephole first."

"I remember." He went to the door, peered out and suddenly opened it with a laugh. "Hello!" he greeted.

Canton Rourke smiled at him. Karie was with him, grinning from ear to ear in her Braves cap and shirt.

"Where's Janine?" Canton asked.

"In Dad's study," he said. "Right through there."

Canton's deep voice had already announced his presence, but Janine felt a jolt somewhere near her heart when she saw him. Two months was so long, she thought. She'd missed him unbearably. Her eyes told him that for her, nothing had changed. She felt the same.

He didn't seem to need words. He smiled tenderly and held out his arms. She got up quickly and ran right into them and lifted her face for a kiss that seemed to have no end at all.

Hectic seconds later, she pressed close, trembling.

"No need to ask if you missed me," he said huskily. "We can get a license in three days, or we can fly down to Mexico and be married in one. Your choice."

"Here," she said immediately. "So that my parents and Kurt can come."

He nodded. "I'd like that, too. I don't have many friends, but the ones I have are the best in the world."

"Mine, too." She reached up and touched his lean cheek. "You look worn."

"I am. It's been a hectic two months. I have my financing and my merger, and Marie is now history."

"What?"

"I flew to Greece with my attorney and had it out with her about Karie," he explained. "Kidnapping is a very serious offense. If I pushed it, the Mexican authorities might find a way to extradite her for trial. She knew it, too. She capitulated without a groan and was willing to settle for what I offered her. She'll have visiting rights, but just between us, I don't think she'll be using them. Karie isn't thrilled at the idea of visiting her at all."

"I remember." She searched his face. "You couldn't have called once?"

He smiled ruefully. "I wanted to be sure you knew who I was."

"I already did," she assured him. "The more I watch the series, the more differences I find between you and my screen hero. I still think he's tops. But I love you," she added shyly, dropping her eyes.

He took a slow breath. "And I love you. Never like this," he added huskily, his eyes brilliant. "Never in my life."

"Me, neither," she agreed breathlessly.

He kissed her again, hungrily, only pausing for breath when young voices came closer.

"Don't tell me," Kurt said dryly when he saw the two of them standing in each other's arms. "The marriage is on again, right?"

"Right," Janine said dreamily.

"Whoopee!" Karie enthused. "Now maybe you'll stop being so grouchy, Dad."

He glared at her.

"Same for you, Janine," Kurt agreed with a grin.

Canton glanced from the children's smug faces to Janine's. "Have you seen the tabloid this week?" he asked, naming one of the biggest ones.

"Yes. Kurt showed it to me," she explained. "It had a sea creature that had washed up on a Mexican beach."

"You didn't recognize it?" He reached into his pocket and unfolded the front page of one, that he'd been carrying around with him. Kurt and Karie looked suddenly restless.

Janine stared at the color photo with a frown. "Well, I thought it was rather familiar..."

"The cow skull?" he prompted. "The hacked-up garden hose? The feathers? The fur?"

She gasped and looked at Kurt with wide eyes. "It can't be!"

Karie cleared her throat. "Now, Dad," she began when his eyes narrowed.

"We covered it up the minute we took the photo," Kurt said helpfully. "The tide would have washed it all out to sea, we made sure of it."

"Why?" he demanded.

Karie pursed her lips, glanced at Kurt and produced a check. "Well, this is why," she explained.

He unfolded the check, made out to his daughter, and almost choked. "You're kidding."

She shook her head. "I wasn't sure you were going to make back all that money you lost," she said. "So I hit on this keen idea. I have to split it with Kurt, of course, but it should get me through college. Gosh, it should get us both through college!"

He was torn between being touched and committing homicide. "This is a hoax! It's all going back, and there will be a retraction printed."

"And I told them so in my letter," she assured him. "I kept a copy of it. They said it didn't matter, it was a super hoax." She put her hand on her hip and struck a pose. "Get real, Dad, do you honestly think Elvis is living on Mars, like they said last week?"

She sounded so old and sophisticated that both of the adults broke up, though Canton was still determined to set things right.

"She's your daughter," Janine said through tears of laughter.

"And yours," he reminded her, "as soon as the ring is on your finger."

"Lucky you," Karie said with an irrepressible grin.

"Lucky me," Kurt agreed. "Just think of all the wonderful times we're going to have together."

Canton and Janine looked at the picture in the tabloid, and then at the children.

"Private schools," Canton said.

"In different states," Janine agreed.

The kids only looked at one another with knowing smiles. Canton took Janine by the hand and led her out of the room, into the office and closed the door behind them.

"Now," he murmured as he took her in his arms. "I believe we were discussing our forthcoming marriage? I think I stopped just about...here."

He bent and kissed her with slow, steady warmth, and she smiled with pure joy under his mouth. And it was no mystery at all that he loved her. Or vice versa.

*   *   *   *   *

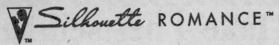

Silhouette ROMANCE™

cordially invites you to the unplanned nuptials
of three unsuspecting hunks and their

SURPRISE BRIDES

Look for the following specially packaged titles:

March 1997: MISSING: ONE BRIDE by Alice Sharpe, #1212
April 1997: LOOK-ALIKE BRIDE by Laura Anthony, #1220
May 1997: THE SECRET GROOM by Myrna Mackenzie, #1225

Don't miss **Surprise Brides**, an irresistible trio of books about love
and marriage by three talented authors! Found only in—

Silhouette ROMANCE™

Take 4 bestselling love stories FREE

Plus get a FREE surprise gift!

Special Limited-time Offer

Mail to Silhouette Reader Service®

P.O. Box 609
Fort Erie, Ontario
L2A 5X3

YES! Please send me 4 free Silhouette Romance™ novels and my free surprise gift. Then send me 6 brand-new novels every month, which I will receive months before they appear in bookstores. Bill me at the low price of $3.00 each plus 25¢ delivery and GST*. That's the complete price and a savings of over 10% off the cover prices—quite a bargain! I understand that accepting the books and gift places me under no obligation ever to buy any books. I can always return a shipment and cancel at any time. Even if I never buy another book from Silhouette, the 4 free books and the surprise gift are mine to keep forever.

315 BPA A3UX

Name	(PLEASE PRINT)	
Address		Apt. No.
City	Province	Postal Code

This offer is limited to one order per household and not valid to present Silhouette Romance™ subscribers. *Terms and prices are subject to change without notice. Canadian residents will be charged applicable provincial taxes and GST.

As seen on TV!
Free Gift Offer

With a Free Gift proof-of-purchase from any Silhouette® book,
you can receive a beautiful cubic zirconia pendant.

This gorgeous marquise-shaped stone is a genuine cubic
zirconia—accented by an 18" gold tone necklace.

(Approximate retail value $19.95)

Send for yours today...
compliments of ▼ *Silhouette*®
TM

To receive your free gift, a cubic zirconia pendant, send us one original proof-of-
purchase, photocopies not accepted, from the back of any Silhouette Romance™,
Silhouette Desire®, Silhouette Special Edition®, Silhouette Intimate Moments®
or Silhouette Yours Truly™ title available in February, March and April at your favorite
retail outlet, together with the Free Gift Certificate, plus a check or money order for
$1.65 U.S./$2.15 CAN. (do not send cash) to cover postage and handling, payable
to Silhouette Free Gift Offer. We will send you the specified gift. Allow 6 to 8 weeks for
delivery. Offer good until April 30, 1997 or while quantities last. Offer valid in the
U.S. and Canada only.

Free Gift Certificate

Name: _____

Address: _____

City: _____ State/Province: _____ Zip/Postal Code: _____

Mail this certificate, one proof-of-purchase and a check or money order for postage
and handling to: SILHOUETTE FREE GIFT OFFER 1997. In the U.S.: 3010 Walden
Avenue, P.O. Box 9077, Buffalo NY 14269-9077. In Canada: P.O. Box 613, Fort Erie,
Ontario L2Z 5X3.

FREE GIFT OFFER   084-KFD
ONE PROOF-OF-PURCHASE
To collect your fabulous FREE GIFT, a cubic zirconia pendant, you must include this
original proof-of-purchase for each gift with the properly completed Free Gift Certificate.

084-KFD

You're About to Become a

Privileged Woman

Reap the rewards of fabulous free gifts and benefits with proofs-of-purchase from Silhouette and Harlequin books

Pages & Privileges™

It's our way of thanking you for buying our books at your favorite retail stores.

Pages & Privileges ™

✂

‖ PROOF OF PURCHASE ‖ SR-PP23
Offer expires March 31, 1997

Harlequin and Silhouette— the most privileged readers in the world!

For more information about Harlequin and Silhouette's PAGES & PRIVILEGES program call the Pages & Privileges Benefits Desk: 1-503-794-2499

SR-PP23